LAURIE HALSE ANDERSON

FEVER
1793

Simon & Schuster Books for Young Readers
New York London Toronto Sydney

SIMON & SCHUSTER BOOKS FOR YOUNG READERS

An imprint of Simon & Schuster Children's Publishing Division

1230 Avenue of the Americas, New York, New York 10020

This book is a work of fiction. Any references to historical events, real people, or real locales are used fictitiously. Other names, characters, places, and incidents are the product of the author's imagination, and any resemblance to actual events or locales or persons, living or dead, is entirely coincidental.

Text copyright © 2000 by Laurie Halse Anderson

All rights reserved including the right of reproduction in whole or in part in any form.

SIMON & SCHUSTER BOOKS FOR YOUNG READERS is a trademark of Simon & Schuster, Inc.

For information about special discounts for bulk purchases, please contact Simon & Schuster Special Sales at 1-866-506-1949 or business@simonandschuster.com. The Simon & Schuster Speakers Bureau can bring authors to your live event. For more information or to book an event, contact the Simon & Schuster Speakers Bureau at 1-866-248-3049 or visit our website at www.simonspeakers.com.

Also available in a hardcover edition.

Book design by Steve Scott

The text for this book is set in Adobe Caslon.

Manufactured in the United States of America

32 34 36 38 40 39 37 35 33

The Library of Congress has cataloged the hardcover edition as follows:

Anderson, Laurie Halse.

Fever 1793 / by Laurie Halse Anderson.

p. cm.

Summary: In 1793 Philadelphia, sixteen-year-old Matilda Cook, separated from her sick mother, learns about perseverance and self-reliance when she is forced to cope with the horrors of a yellow fever epidemic.

ISBN 978-0-689-83858-3 (hc)

[1. Yellow fever—Pennsylvania—Philadelphia—Fiction. 2. Epidemics—Fiction. 3. Pennsylvania—History—1775-1865—Fiction. 4. Philadelphia (Pa.)—Fiction. 5. Survival—Fiction.] I. Title

PZ7.A5438Fe 2000 [Fic]—dc21 00-032238

ISBN 978-0-689-84891-9 (pbk)

0413 OFF

This book is for my father,
Reverend Frank A. Halse Jr,
the finest man I know.
—L. H. A.

CHAPTER ONE

August 16th, 1793

*The city of Philadelphia is perhaps one of
the wonders of the world.*
—Lord Adam Gordon
Journal entry, 1765

I woke to the sound of a mosquito whining in my left ear and my mother screeching in the right.

"Rouse yourself this instant!"

Mother snapped open the shutters and heat poured into our bedchamber. The room above our coffeehouse was not large. Two beds, a washstand, and a wooden trunk with frayed leather straps nearly filled it. It seemed even smaller with Mother storming around.

"Get out of bed, Matilda," she continued. "You're sleeping the day away." She shook my shoulder. "Polly's late and there's work to be done."

The noisy mosquito darted between us. I started to sweat under the thin blanket. It was going to be another hot August day. Another long, hot August day. Another long, hot, boring, wretched August day.

"I can't tell who is lazier, Polly or you," Mother muttered as she stalked out of the room. "When I was a girl, we were up before the sun . . ." Her voice droned on and on as she clattered down the stairs.

I groaned. Mother had been a perfect girl. Her family was wealthy then, but that didn't stop her from stitching entire quilts before breakfast, or spinning miles of wool before tea. It was the War, she liked to remind me. Children did what was asked of them. And she never complained. Oh, no, never. Good children were seen and not heard. How utterly unlike me.

I yawned and stretched, then snuggled back onto my pillow. A few more minutes' rest, that's what I needed. I'd float back to sleep, drifting like Blanchard's giant yellow balloon. I could just see it: the winter's day, the crowds on the rooftops, the balloon tugging at its ropes. I held my breath. Would the ropes break?

The devilish mosquito attacked, sinking its needle-nose into my forehead.

"Ow!"

I leapt from my bed, and—*thunk!*—cracked my head on the sloped ceiling. The ceiling was lower than it used to be. Either that, or I had grown another inch overnight. I sat back down, wide awake now, my noggin sporting two lumps—one from the ceiling, one from the mosquito.

No balloon trips for me.

To work, then. I got to my feet and crossed the room, ducking my head cautiously. The water in the washbasin was cloudy, and the facecloth smelled like old cheese. I decided to clean up later, perhaps next December.

A squeaking mouse dashed by my toes, followed by a flash of orange fur named Silas. The mouse ran to a corner, its claws scratching desperately on the floorboards. Silas pounced. The squeaking stopped.

"Oh, Silas! Did you have to do that?"

Silas didn't answer. He rarely did. Instead he jumped up on Mother's quilt and prepared to pick apart his breakfast.

Mother's best quilt. Mother abhorred mice.

I sprang across the room. "Get down!" I commanded.

Silas hissed at me but obeyed, leaping to the floor and padding out the door.

"Matilda?" Mother's voice called up the stairs. "Now!"

I made a face at the doorway. I had just saved her precious quilt from disaster, but would she appreciate it? Of course not.

No more dawdling. I had to get dressed.

I fastened my stays and a badly embroidered pocket over the white shift I slept in. Then I stepped into my blue linen skirt. It nearly showed my ankles. Along with the ceiling getting lower, my clothes were shrinking, too.

Once dressed, I faced the rather dead mouse and wrinkled my nose. Picking it up by the tail, I carried the corpse to the front window and leaned out.

My city, Philadelphia, was wide awake. My heart beat faster and my head cleared. Below the window, High Street teemed with horsemen, carriages, and carts. I could hear Mrs. Henning gossiping on her front stoop and dogs barking at a pig running loose in the street.

The sound of the blacksmith's hammer on his anvil reminded me of Polly, our tardy serving girl. That's where she was, no doubt; in the blacksmith's shop, eyeing Matthew, the blacksmith's son. I didn't like it there. The roaring furnace, sparks crackling in the air, the sizzle of hot metal into cold water—it all reminded me of that unmentionable place the preachers liked to go on about.

My favorite place was the waterfront. I squinted eastward. The rooftop of the State House, where the Congress met, was visible, but the August haze and dust from the street made it impossible to see farther than that. On a clear day, I could see the masts of the ships tied up at the wharves on the Delaware River. I promised myself a secret visit to the docks later, as soon as Polly arrived to distract Mother.

A few blocks south lay the Walnut Street Prison, where Blanchard had flown that remarkable balloon. From the prison's courtyard it rose, a yellow silk bubble escaping the earth. I vowed to do that one day, slip free of the ropes that held me. Nathaniel Benson had heard me say it, but he did not laugh. He understood. Perhaps I would see him at the docks, sketching a ship or sea gulls. It had been a long time since we talked.

But before I went anywhere, there was a dead mouse to dispose of. I couldn't throw it into High Street; it might spook one of the horses. I crossed the room and opened the back window overlooking the garden. Maybe Silas would smell his treat out there and get a decent breakfast after all. I flung the corpse as far as I could, then hurried downstairs before Mother boiled over.

CHAPTER TWO

August 16th, 1793

*. . . the first and most principal to be, a perfect
skill and knowledge in cookery . . . because it
is a duty well belonging to women.*
—Gervase Markham
The English House Wife, 1668

As soon as I stepped into the kitchen, Mother started
her lecture.

"Too much sleep is bad for your health, Matilda."
She slipped a freshly made ball of butter into a stone
crock. "It must be a grippe, a sleeping sickness."

I tried not to listen to her. I had not cleared the wax
from my ears all summer, hoping it would soften her
voice. It had not worked.

"You should be dosed with fish oil. When I was a
girl . . ." She kept talking to herself as she carried a
steaming pot of water outside to rinse the butter churn.

I sat down at the table. Our kitchen was larger than
most, with an enormous hearth crowded with pots and

kettles, and two bake ovens built into the brickwork beside it. The size of the room did not match the size of our family. We were only three: Mother, Grandfather, and me, plus Eliza who worked for us. But the roomy kitchen could feed one hundred people in a day. My family owned the Cook Coffeehouse. The soon-to-be famous Cook Coffeehouse, Grandfather liked to say.

My father had built our home and business after the War for Independence ended in 1783. I was four years old. The coffeehouse sat just off the corner of Seventh and High Streets. At first we were lucky if a lost farmer strayed in, but business improved when President Washington's house was built two blocks away.

Father was a carpenter by trade, and he built us a sturdy home. The room where we served customers filled most of the first floor and had four large windows. The kitchen was tucked into the back, filled with useful shelves and built-in cupboards to store things. We could have used a sitting room, truth be told. Father would have added one on if he had lived. But he fell off a ladder and died of a broken neck two months after the coffeehouse opened. That's when Grandfather joined us.

A coffeehouse was a respectable business for a widow and her father-in-law to run. Mother refused to serve spirits, but she allowed card games and a small bit of gambling as long as she didn't have to see it. By midday the front room was usually crowded with gentlemen, merchants, and politicians enjoying a cup of coffee, a bite to eat, and the news of the day. Father would have been proud. I wondered what he would have thought of me.

"Good morning," Eliza said loudly, startling me. "I thought you were going to sleep the day away. Have you eaten?" She set a sack of coffee beans on the table.

"I'm starving," I said, clutching my stomach.

"As usual," she said with a smile. "Let me get you something quick."

Eliza was the coffeehouse cook. Mother couldn't prepare a meal fit for pigs. I found this amusing, considering our last name was Cook. In a manner, though, it was serious. If not for Eliza's fine victuals, and the hungry customers who paid to eat them, we'd have been in the streets long ago. Mother's family had washed their hands of her when she ran off to marry a carpenter, a tradesman (the horror!), when she was but seventeen. So we were very fond of Eliza.

Like most blacks in Philadelphia, Eliza was free. She said Philadelphia was the best city for freed slaves or freeborn Africans. The Quakers here didn't hold with slavery and tried hard to convince others that slavery was against God's will. Black people were treated different than white people, that was plain to see, but Eliza said nobody could tell her what to do or where to go, and no one would ever, ever beat her again.

She had been born a slave near Williamsburg, Virginia. Her husband saved up his horseshoeing money and bought her freedom right after they were married. She told me that was the best day of her life. She moved to Philadelphia and cooked for us, saving her wages to set her husband free.

When I was eight, she got a letter saying her husband had been killed by a runaway horse. That was her worst day. She didn't say a word for months. My father had only been dead two years, so Mother knew just what lay in Eliza's heart. They both supped sorrow with a big spoon, that's what Mother said. It took years, but the smile slowly returned to Eliza's face. She didn't turn sour like Mother did.

Eliza was the luckiest person I knew. She got to walk from the river past shop windows, market stalls, and the courthouse up to Seventh Street every morning. She told stories even better than Grandfather, and she knew how to keep a secret. She laughed once when I told her she was my best friend, but it was the truth.

She dished up a bowl of oatmeal from a pot that hung by the side of the hearth, then carefully set it in front of me. "Eat up," she said. One corner of her mouth turned up just a bit and she winked.

I tasted the oatmeal. It was sweet. Eliza had hidden a sugar lump at the bottom of the bowl.

"Thank you," I whispered.

"You're welcome," she whispered back.

"Why is Polly late?" I asked. "Have you seen her?"

Eliza shook her head. "Your mother is in a lather, I

promise you," she warned. "If Polly doesn't get here soon, she may need to find herself another position."

"I bet she's dawdling by the forge," I said, "watching Matthew work with his shirt collar open."

"Maybe she's ill," Eliza said. "There's talk of sickness by the river."

Mother strode into the room carrying wood for the fire.

"Serving girls don't get sick," Mother said. "If she doesn't appear soon, you'll have to do her chores as well as your own, Matilda. And where is your grandfather? I sent him to inquire about a box of tea an hour ago. He should have returned by now."

"I'd be happy to search for him," I offered. "I could look for Polly, too."

Mother added wood to the fire, poking the logs until the flames jumped. The delicate tip of her shoe tapped impatiently. "No. I'll go. If Father comes back, don't let him leave. And Matilda, see to the garden."

She quickly tied a bonnet under her chin and left, the back door closing behind her with the sharp sound of a musket shot.

"Well," said Eliza. "That's it, then. Here, have some veal and corn bread. Seems like you've a long day ahead of you."

After she cut me two slices of cold veal and a thick piece of fresh corn bread, Eliza started to make ginger-bread, one of her specialties. Nutmeg and cinnamon perfumed the air as she ground the spices with a pestle. If not for the heat, I could have stayed in the kitchen for an eternity. The house was silent except for the popping of the applewood in the fire, and the tall clock ticking in the front room. I took a sip from a half-filled mug on the table.

"Ugh! It's coffee!" Black coffee, bitter as medicine. "How can you drink this?" I asked Eliza.

"It tastes better if you don't steal it," she answered. She took the cup from my hands. "Pour your own and leave mine be."

"Are we out of cider?" I asked. "I could get some at the marketplace."

"Oh, no," Eliza said. "You'll stay right here. Your mother needs your help, and that poor garden is like to expire. It is time for you to haul some water, little Mattie."

Little Mattie indeed. Another month and I'd be almost as tall as Eliza. I hated to be called "little."

I sighed loudly, put my dishes in the washtub, and tucked my hair into my mob cap. I tied a disreputable straw hat atop the cap, one I could never wear in the street, and snatched a bite of dough from Eliza's bowl before I ran outside.

The garden measured fifty paces up one side and twenty along the other, but after six weeks of drought it seemed as long and wide as a city block, filled with thousands of drooping plants crying for help.

I dropped the bucket into the well to fill it with water, then turned the handle to bring it back up again. Little Mattie, indeed. I was big enough to be ordered around like an unpaid servant. Big enough for mother to grumble about finding me a husband.

I carried the water to the potato patch and poured it out too fast. Big enough to plan for the day when I would no longer live here.

If I was going to work as hard as a mule, it might as well be for my own benefit. I was going to travel to France and bring back fabric and combs and jewelry that the ladies of Philadelphia would swoon over. And that was just for the dry goods store. I wanted to own an entire city block—a proper restaurant, an apothecary, maybe a school, or a hatter's shop. Grandfather said I was a Daughter of Liberty, a real American girl. I could steer my own ship. No one would call me little Mattie. They would call me "Ma'am."

"Dash it all." I had watered a row of weeds.

As I returned to the well, Mother came through the garden gate.

"Where's Polly?" I asked as I dropped the bucket down the well. "Did you pass by the blacksmith's?"

"I spoke with her mother, with Mistress Logan," Mother answered softly, looking at her neat rows of carrots.

"And?" I waved a mosquito away from my face.

"It happened quickly. Polly sewed by candlelight

after dinner. Her mother repeated that over and over, 'she sewed by candlelight after dinner.' And then she collapsed."

I released the handle and the bucket splashed, a distant sound.

"Matilda, Polly's dead."

CHAPTER THREE

August 16th, 1793

Oh then the hands of the pitiful Mother
prepared her Child's body for the grave . . .
—Letter of Margaret Morris
Philadelphia, 1793

D ead? Polly's dead?" I couldn't have heard her properly. "Polly Logan?" The sweat on my neck turned to ice and I shivered. "Our Polly? That can't be."

I tried to remember the last time we had played together. It was before she started working for us. Last Christmas—no, well before that. Her family had moved to Third Street at least two years ago. She had been a cradle friend, the girl I played dolls with. We sang nonsense songs together when we churned butter. I could see it then, my small hands and Polly's together on the handle of the churn. I took a deep breath and closed my eyes.

Mother led me inside by the elbow and I sat heavily on a chair. She quickly told Eliza what happened.

"There was no doctor in attendance," Mother

explained. "She shook with fever briefly, three quarters of an hour, cried out once, and died in her own bed. They don't know what it was."

"It could have been anything. There are so many fevers at summer's end," Eliza said. "Is anyone else in the house sick?"

"Sick with grief," Mother said. She poured herself and Eliza each a mug of coffee. "It's a large family, she still has seven children under ten years, one a babe in her arms."

"We'll pray they don't take sick," Eliza said as she took the mug. "Are any neighbors ill?"

Mother blew in her cup and nodded. "An old man who lives across the alley is rumored to be sick in bed, but you know how these stories catch fire. It's strange though. She was a healthy girl, robust. Never saw her so much as sneeze before."

I kept my eyes closed, trying to see Polly happy, joking, maybe stealing a kiss with Matthew, then bursting through the door to tell me. It couldn't be real. How could Polly be dead?

"Matilda, are you well?" asked Mother. "She looks peculiar, don't you think, Eliza? Are you feverish?" She laid her hand on my forehead. Her fingers were rough but cool, and smelled faintly of lavender. I wanted to lay my head on her shoulder, but that would have been awkward.

Mother slipped her hand to the back of my neck.

"She did not suffer, Matilda. We must be grateful for that." She removed her hand and peered into my eyes. "This heat is not healthy. You must tell me straight away if you feel peckish."

I waited for her to say something more about Polly. She did not.

"We should send along something for the family," suggested Eliza. "Her mother is in no condition to cook. Mattie could take a ham over."

"No," Mother said quickly. She set the coffee mug on the table with a thump. "I don't want her near there, not with a sickness in the air. Besides, she hasn't played with Polly for years. The girl was our servant, not a friend."

"Yes, she was," I protested. "Let me go, please. I'll take some food, you know they need it, and I'll pay my respects to her mother. It's the proper thing to do."

"I've already paid our respects," Mother said. "You'll just upset her mother more. I'll take a food basket there myself. Tomorrow. Now put on a clean apron, Matilda, and wash your hands. It's time to get to work."

"I want to see her!"

"No."

"What about the funeral?" I asked, blinking back the tears. "You must let me attend that."

"No. Absolutely not. I forbid it. You'll have nightmares."

"She was my friend! You must allow me. Why are you so horrid?"

As soon as the angry words were out of my mouth, I knew I had gone too far.

"Matilda!" Mother rose from her chair. "You are forbidden to speak to me in that tone! Apologize at once."

The sun coming in the south window cast deep shadows under her eyes and cheekbones. She held her jaw tight, her eyes flashing with anger. She looked old, much older than she should. She hadn't always been so pinch-faced and harsh.

When Mother allowed herself a still moment by the fire on winter nights, I could sometimes see the face she wore when Father was alive. Back then Mother smiled at me with her eyes and her laughter and her gentle hands. But no longer. Life was a battle, and Mother a tired and bitter captain. The captain I had to obey.

"My apologies," I said.

CHAPTER FOUR

August 16th, 1793

Diet Bread: One pound sugar, 9 eggs, beat for an hour, add to 14 ounces flour, teaspoon rosewater, one teaspoon cinnamon or coriander, bake quick.

—Amelia Simmons
American Cookbook, 1796

By midafternoon the front room of the coffeehouse was thick with customers, pipe smoke, and loud arguments. A ship's captain finished telling a yarn, and the windowpanes rattled with laughter. Mother poured him a cup of coffee with a steady hand. She looked up as I walked by carrying a tray of fresh gingerbread, but she wouldn't meet my eye.

"Over here, lass!" Grandfather shouted from his corner seat. Above his head hung the cage of King George, the scraggly green parrot won in a card game. "Bring those delectables over here and give us a kiss."

My Grandfather was Captain William Farnsworth

Cook of the Pennsylvania Fifth Regiment. He was a stout man, thanks to Eliza's cooking, and the heart of all gossip and tall tales in the coffeehouse. He had been an army officer his whole life, and was happiest when serving under General Washington. He tried to instill some military training in me, but always sweetened it with candy.

I held the tray over my head as I squeezed past the crowded tables. Grandfather sat with two government officials, a lawyer, and Mr. Carris, who owned an export business. I set the tray in front of Grandfather, and he patted my hand.

"Look here, gentlemen, sweets offered by the sweetest filly in the Commonwealth. What will you have?"

"Can that be little Mattie?" elderly Mr. Carris asked as he squinted through his bifocals. "Why, she's grown into a fine young lady. Much too fine for this type of work. We'll have to find a husband for you."

"A husband! A husband!" King George squawked.

My face flushed as the men laughed.

"Hush, you old thing," I muttered to the bird. It would have been rude to hush Mr. Carris. "I'll feed you to Silas if you don't close that beak."

Grandfather gave the pest a piece of gingerbread, and Mr. Carris went back to his original subject.

"It's that heap of rotting coffee beans on Ball's Wharf, I tell you," Mr. Carris said to the other men. "It's the source of a deadly miasma, a foul stench, indeed.

There are noxious fumes all around the district. Mark my words, it will be a killer yet."

Is that what killed Polly? A miasma? I could feel the tears stinging my eyes, but I couldn't escape, not with Grandfather holding my hand. I wanted to tell him what happened; he'd understand. But not in front of all these people.

The lawyer shook his head in disagreement.

"It creates an awful stench, yes, but no one dies from a bad smell. If they did, every farmer spreading manure would be long dead and us city-dwellers all hungry!"

Grandfather roared with laughter and slapped his knee.

"Hungry," echoed King George.

"Hold there, Marks, hold there, I say," interjected the government clerk. His left eye blinked with a nervous twitch. "I've heard stories of a fever among the Santo Domingan refugees. They live close to Ball's Wharf, you know."

A doctor at the next table looked up from his backgammon board and interrupted the conversation.

"It is not just the refugees," the doctor said. "This morning I spoke with a colleague who was called to the Shewall home. Mary Shewall died soon after of a bilious fever, and one could hardly fault her character. There may well be a disease in the air again. Yellow fever."

The room grew quiet as the entire company listened in.

"A woman dies of some illness and you talk of yellow fever?" the lawyer asked. "We haven't seen yellow fever in Philadelphia for thirty years."

"It is too early to tell," the doctor agreed. "But I know of some who are sending their wives and children up to the country, to healthful air and cool breezes."

"You doctors are all alike, scaring us to earn more business. My family will stay right where they are, thank you," the lawyer replied.

"All the same, a trip to the country sounds refreshing," Mr. Carris said.

Grandfather thumped his boot on the floor.

"Balderdash! Bad coffee is a nuisance, but it won't kill anyone. Some poor soul dies of a fever every August. That's why my boy had the good sense to open this fine establishment so far away from the river, away from the smells, filth, and disease. Enough fever talk. Mattie girl, bring us more tea. And who will tell me why Mr. Jefferson wants to quit his job? Isn't being secretary of state good enough for him? Or does he want something more?"

The men all shouted. They loved to argue about Mr. Jefferson.

I fetched a fresh pot of coffee from the kitchen. Eliza and Mother didn't say a word to me; there was too much work to do. I poured coffee and tea, served oyster loaf and Indian pudding, carried the dirty dishes back to Eliza, and tried to keep the floor swept clean. I didn't have time to worry about fevers or husbands or rude parrots.

Eventually the hour struck and the customers donned their hats and said their farewells. Mother called me to help figure the bills and exchange the many kinds of money: pence from Massachusetts, shillings from Virginia, British pounds, and French francs.

I double-checked the long column of numbers. Taking care of accounts was one territory that Mother conceded to me. If she added the fingers on one hand, she was just as likely to total four as six.

Grandfather left for his constitutional stroll around the city, but I was not allowed to join him. I had to take Polly's place in the kitchen, washing up, sweeping the floors, dusting the tables, and putting everything back in its proper place so we would be ready to do the same thing the next day.

My arms felt as heavy as lead from carrying the trays. My shift was sticky with perspiration, and I smelled of tobacco smoke and unwashed strangers. How did Polly do this every day?

I forced my eyes open to look at Mother putting away the clean china.

"I'll help," I said.

"Don't be ridiculous," she answered. "You're exhausted. Polly will do it in the morning."

She stopped. The house was silent for a moment, except for the sound of Matthew down the block still hammering away at his forge. Had anyone told him that Polly was gone?

"I'll finish it," Mother corrected herself. "Go to bed. I need you up early to clean out the fireplace."

CHAPTER FIVE

August 24th, 1793

A low voice and soft address are the common
indications of a well-bred woman.
—Hannah More
The Young Lady Abroad or Affectionate
Advice on the Social and Moral Habits
of Females, 1777

A week later, sixty-four people had died, though no one seemed quite sure what killed them. Rumors of a fever near the docks snaked through the city. People avoided the shops by the river and came up to our end of High Street, where the air smelled cleaner. They made our strongbox grow delightfully heavy.

There was little time to mourn for Polly. I slaved from dawn until the stars shone: house chores in the morning, serving coffee in the afternoon, and cleaning after supper. Sleep became more precious to me than food. One night, I fell asleep in the necessary and woke with a fervent prayer of thanks that I had not fallen in.

My first chance for escape came eight days after Polly died, as Mother and Grandfather discussed their plans for the day.

"We need extra eggs, hard cheese, pippin apples, and savory. And lemons. I'll have to go to the market again," sighed Mother. I concentrated on a hoe cake spread thick with honey.

"You're too tired, Lucille. Send the child to market," Grandfather suggested.

I quickly swallowed the hoe cake.

"No, Matilda must stay home. I shall go." Mother fanned herself with her hand. "It is uncommonly warm, isn't it?"

I jumped to my feet.

"Grandfather's right, you need the rest. Please let me go."

Mother tapped her finger on the table, a good sign. She was thinking.

Grandfather tried again.

"You've fussed for days because you don't like her serving customers. Let her run the market errands. It will clear her head. Young people need the outside air."

The fingers stopped. A bad sign.

"I was thinking of sending her to the country, to the Ludingtons at Gwynedd. You encourage her to go deeper into town." Mother frowned.

The Ludingtons? The Ludingtons had a farm with disgusting pigs and dogs that bit. Any place would be better than the Ludingtons.

Grandfather fed a cracker to King George.

"Must you be so gloomy, woman? You see darkness in every corner. Sending her away—your own child? You shock me. The Ludingtons aren't even family. I can't see the wisdom in that. We'll have to consider this at some length," he said, drawing out his pipe.

The considering could take hours. The sun was growing hotter and the larder stood empty.

"If I don't go soon, everything will be sold or spoiled," I reminded them. "People don't stop eating eggs whenever there's a fever, do they?" I had to get her attention away from that farm.

"The child's right, Lucille. She'll be fine. We must accommodate our lives to the fever for a few weeks, but we shan't overthrow our daily routines. It's important that we not lose our heads."

"But Polly . . ." Mother started.

"Whatever took that little imp away, it wasn't a fever, I promise you that," Grandfather said. "It could have been a sudden pleurisy or a weak heart. You worry too much. Always have. The market is the safest place in town, next to our own castle here. Now let the child get some air."

Mother pursed her lips a moment, then nodded. "I'll write a list for you."

"I know what we need," I quickly replied.

"Don't shop at any stalls below Third Street. Stay

away from Second Street Market completely. And no rambles today. You go to the market and then you come home. And do not let me hear of you loitering shamelessly in front of the Peale house."

I turned so she would not see me blush. Why did it matter if I walked past the Peales'? "I think we should buy extra bread at the Simmons' bakery. We're sure to run out again."

"Good idea, girl," said Grandfather. "See there, Lucille. The child minds the shop as well as you. You mustn't be so hard on her. Come here, Mattie, give this old soldier a kiss."

I pecked his cheek and he slipped a piece of hard candy into my hand. I dashed out the door before Mother could change her mind.

As I crossed Fourth Street, the noise from the market splashed over me like a wave.

"'Ere's yer lily-white hot corn! Get your nice hot corn!"

"Fresh fish fit for the pan!"

"Raaaaaaspberries! Blaaaaaaackberries!"

"Pepperpot! All hot! Makee strong! Makee live long! Come buy my pepperpot!"

The market stalls stretched for three blocks in the center of the street. West Indian women stood by their pepperpot kettles stirring fragrant stews, while the hot corn girls walked up and down the street. The distant call of the charcoal man's horn sounded at the far end of the market. Chickens clucked and geese honked, customers argued about the price of pears, and children ran everywhere.

Eggs, pippins, savory, what else did she want? I thought. Cabbage? Crab apples? I rolled the candy in my mouth. It had a piece of tobacco stuck to it from Grandfather's pocket. I spit it out and walked up to the egg sellers.

"Hello, Miss Matilda Cook!"

"Good morning, Mrs. Epler."

Mr. and Mrs. Epler were German farmers who brought their eggs and chickens to market three times a week. Mrs. Epler fluttered in her stall, her tiny black eyes looking this way and that, her chins flapping as she spoke. Mr. Epler was egg-shaped; narrow at the top and bottom, bulging in the middle. He never spoke.

His wife leaned forward.

"I was just telling Epler here that your people would be already gone. All the farmers talk, talk, talk of this fever." She waved her arms, scaring the chickens in their wooden pens at her feet. "So much fever talk!"

"Don't you believe it?" I asked.

"Them that are sick should the church visit. City folk, sinners at the docks. They don't visit the church, and God gives them the fever. It is a sign from God. The Bible says the soul that sinneth, it shall die."

Mr. Epler nodded his head solemnly.

"Did you to church go last week, Miss Matilda Cook?" Mrs. Epler leaned her beak forward.

"Yes, Ma'am. Mother never lets me stay home."

Mrs. Epler's face broke into a wide grin.

"She's a good woman, your mother. You go to church and you have no worries! How many eggs you want, *liebchen*?"

With the eggs carefully tucked in my basket, I moved on to Mr. Owens's stall. He wrung his hands and apologized for the sorry-looking cabbages.

"We were lucky to get those, what with this drought and all," he said.

He was so discouraged about the cabbages, it was easy to talk his price down. He may have lowered it even further, but I felt sorry for him. He had more children on his farm than he could count on two hands. (The extra money was just what I needed to buy a bag of hard candy. Without tobacco specks.)

The next stall had fresh lemons. I scratched the peel and held one up to my nose. Paris would smell like a lemon peel, far away and wonderful. I bought a dozen and kept one in my hand as I shopped.

There was no savory to be found, and the apples were small and knobbly. Mrs. Hotchkiss charged an outrageous price for a moldy cheese, but there were no other cheese sellers. I had to use all the hard candy money. I did not bid her good day.

As I rounded the butcher's stall at the far end of the

market, someone grabbed my basket and spun me around. I clenched my fists and whirled to face my assailant.

Nathaniel Benson.

My stomach flipped over like an egg in a skillet. I brushed my hands on my apron.

"Little Mattie is come to market. Are you sure you haven't lost your way?" he teased.

Nathaniel Benson.

He looked much more a man and less a boy than he had a few months earlier. He had sprouted up over my head and grown broad in the chest. Stop, I cautioned myself. You shouldn't look at him as if he were a race-horse for sale. But his hair was a beautiful chestnut color. . . .

I often walked past the Peales' house, but rarely had the chance to speak with him. His work as a painter's assistant required long hours. He was known to stroll past the coffeehouse from time to time, but Mother kept me busy when he approached. He wasn't suitable, she said. Had no future, was a scamp, possibly even a scoundrel.

Last New Year's Day, Nathaniel had rubbed snow in my face and chased me across the ice. I pushed him into a snowbank, and Mother sent me home in disgrace. The following week, he took me to watch Blanchard's balloon fly away. He thought it would be marvelous to visit Paris.

Nathaniel Benson.

I cleared my throat.

"Good afternoon, Nathaniel. Kindly return my basket."

"Is that all you have to say? You disappoint me. I thought you would send me sailing into the horse trough at least. I guess you respect my new position as a man of the world."

"You are not a man of the world, you clean paintbrushes, though for the life of me I don't know why Mr. Peale bothers with you. And you will end up in that trough if you don't give back my basket." I paused. "Your shoe buckle is missing."

"What?"

I grabbed the basket as he looked down to inspect his shoe.

"Very funny," he said.

"Why are you here?" I asked. "Shouldn't you be working?"

He snatched an apple from my basket and took a bite. The impudence.

"Master Peale gave me the day off. He has a committee meeting with the mayor and a visit with a banker. I ruin so much when he's present, he's afraid to let me work unsupervised. The day is mine, so I'm going fishing. Want to come?"

Fishing. I hadn't been fishing in months. And I'd known Nathaniel since I was a baby, so I could roll my sleeves up above my elbows in his presence. As long as Mother didn't see me do it.

He raised an eyebrow and his eyes sparkled.

"Trout?"

He smiled and I got a chill. When had he started smiling at me like that? Maybe I wouldn't roll up my sleeves. One had to be careful with elbows and boys. I would fish like a lady, with good posture and a demure manner. I could set the eggs in the stream so they wouldn't spoil. . . .

Bong. Bong. Bong.

The bell at Christ Church tolled heavily.

"Why is that ringing?" asked Nathaniel. "It's not the hour."

Bong. Bong. Bong.

A little boy sitting on the cobblestones covered his ears. The chattering marketplace voices hushed as the ringing continued. Every face turned toward the bell swaying in its tower.

"Another person dead," said the butcher. He brought his cleaver down, slicing the mutton leg on his table into two pieces. "The bell rings once for each year the person lived," he explained.

"Nineteen, twenty, twenty-one," counted Nathaniel. The bell stopped. "Twenty-one years old. Do you reckon it was a fever victim?"

"Don't you start carrying on about this fever," I warned. "When Mother isn't hollering at me about something I've done wrong, she's moaning about the fever." I lowered my voice. "Did you hear about Polly Logan?"

He nodded. "Hard to believe, isn't it? I recall you pummeled me once when I stole Polly's doll."

I remembered, too. She loved that doll. I turned away so he couldn't see my tears.

Nathaniel put his hand on my shoulder. "I'm sorry. I didn't mean to make you cry."

His hand felt kind and warm. "I miss her. I didn't even get to say good-bye." I wiped my eyes on my sleeve and cleared my throat again. "Enough about that. We won't talk about it anymore."

"Suit yourself."

Nathaniel stuck his hands in his pockets and stared at the cobblestones. I balanced the basket on my hip. Conversation started up around us as the last echo of the bell died.

"You won't catch anything," I said. "Fish don't bite this time of day."

Nathaniel grunted. He knew I was right. "Well," he started.

"I must go," I interrupted. "There is so much to do at the coffeehouse. Good luck with your paints."

I curtsied awkwardly, stepping on my shift and nearly falling on my face. Nathaniel tipped his hat to me like a gentleman. I tried to walk away with my head held high. I could still feel the weight of his hand on my shoulder.

Good luck with your paints? Did I really say that? What a ninny.

CHAPTER SIX

August 30th, 1793

Directions to the housemaid: Always when you sweep a room, throw a little wet sand all over it, and that will gather up all the flue and dust.

—Hannah Glasse
The Art of Cookery, 1747

I 'll never complain about a cold day again," I vowed after another week of unceasing heat. Grandfather watched from the shade as I cranked the wheel of the mangle. "Do you remember how thick the river ice was New Year's Day?"

Grandfather patted his pockets absentmindedly. Silas crouched next to his chair, intently watching a quivering cherry branch.

"I remember how many cords of firewood I carried and how the wash water by my bed froze every night. No, thank you, Madam, I'd rather a warm day than a cold one. My bones ache at the thought of another frost. Have you seen my pipe?"

I threaded another wet tablecloth through the mangle to squeeze the water from it. The flagstones were cool beneath my bare feet, but the sun burned red as it mounted the sky. Another oppressively hot day.

"No, I haven't seen your pipe. And I adore winter. My favorite part was skating around the ships locked in solid by the ice. The Bensons were there, and the Peales, remember? It was delightful."

Grandfather's white eyebrows crept skyward. "Speaking of Mr. Nathaniel Benson," he started.

"Were we?" I inquired.

"Your mother heard that the young man was behaving improperly toward you at the market."

I let go of the mangle. It swung around and hit me in the leg.

"Ouch. No, I mean. Nathaniel was a gentleman. He expressed his condolences on the death of Polly Logan."

Grandfather coughed once. "Better he should express himself into a better apprenticeship. He'll come of nothing dabbling in Peale's paint pots."

The tablecloth came out the other end of the mangle, and I dropped it into a hickory basket. I waved at the bugs hovering above my head. "I do not wish to discuss Nathaniel Benson. That market is full of busybodies," I grumbled.

"You are right about that. Let me help you, girl." Grandfather rose stiffly. We each took a handle of the basket and carried it to the clotheshorse, a rope strung between two wooden frames that we used for drying clothes and linens. Silas crept to the base of the cherry tree, tail twitching, head steady.

Eliza came through the gate as we spread the table-cloth over the line to dry.

"She certainly has you busy," Eliza chuckled.

"All of us," answered Grandfather. "Look there." He pointed to two sacks by the back door. "She sent me to fetch those Arabica beans! Me, the hero of Trenton and Germantown reduced to a simple errand boy. What has the world come to?"

"Father! Are you trying to kill us all?" my mother yelled from a kitchen window. "Your pipe is near to burn a hole in the table. And where are those coffee beans? We'll have customers soon."

"Some days I'd rather face the British again than listen to the sound of my dear daughter-in-law," Grandfather said. "Ho! Look at that cat."

Silas's tail shot up like a warning flag. He had sighted the enemy—a squirrel. It scampered down the cherry's trunk and ran between Grandfather and Eliza.

Silas leapt to the chase. They raced twice around the garden and under the mangle. The squirrel scrambled up the side of the necessary to the roof. Silas slowed for a heartbeat, then leapt to the fence to gain access to the roof and his furry meal. The squirrel jumped to the ground, and dashed back across the yard, intent on his cherry tree.

"Who wants to wager against the cat?" asked Grandfather. "I say he'll have squirrel soup for his supper."

Silas closed in on the bushy tail. The squirrel lurched left and made a desperate leap up onto my clean laundry. Silas followed. The clotheshorse collapsed under the weight of the stupid beast, sending angry cat and white linen into the red dust.

"Hey!" I hollered.

Silas yowled. Eliza and Grandfather burst into laughter.

"Very droll," I said.

The midday meal was near over by the time I had rewashed the tablecloths. Cold chicken, crisp pickles, butter biscuits, and peach pie were laid out on the table. Mother and Grandfather were on their second mugs of apple cider when I finally sat down.

"What do you think we should do with our extra earnings, Mattie?" Grandfather asked.

"I beg your pardon, Sir?"

"Your grandfather has the foolish notion that we should go into trade," explained Mother. "Open a regular store for the hordes of people who are going to settle at this end of the city any day now."

"No need for a mocking tone, Lucille. We should use our windfall to improve our prospects. If it were up to you, we'd bury the money in the backyard to benefit the worms."

Mother pressed her lips together tightly and set a second piece of chicken on my plate. "Eat," she instructed. "You've worked hard. I don't want you getting sick."

I pushed the chicken to the side. I had plenty of ideas about running the coffeehouse, all of them different from Mother's.

"First we should buy another coffee urn, to serve customers with more haste," I said. I pointed a pickle toward the north wall. "Next is to expand into Mr. Watson's lot. That way, we could offer proper meals, not just tidbits and rolls. You could serve roasts and mutton chops. And we could have an upstairs meeting room for the gentlemen, like the coffeehouses by the wharves."

I took a bite of the pickle.

"And we could reserve space to sell paintings, and combs, and fripperies from France."

"Paintings? Fripperies?" asked Grandfather.

"There is no use talking of expansion, either of you," Mother said. "Our custom improves because business by the docks declines. It's the talk of fever. People are afraid to venture out by the river."

"Philadelphia suffers fevers every August," said Grandfather. "This season it's those cursed refugees. They brought it, just as the ships from Barbados brought it thirty years ago. The mayor should quarantine them on Hog Island for a few weeks and the fever would pass." He lifted his mug to King George. The parrot drank.

"Must you encourage that creature?" Mother asked. "Perhaps we should leave, just until the weather breaks. Elizabeth Bachel's family left this morning."

"I say we keep our heads and turn a tidy profit," Grandfather continued. "Let others flee. We Cooks are made of stronger stuff!"

"Be that as it may, the increased profits are temporary," said Mother. "The fever will pass and these new customers will go back to the wharves. If we do save some money, we'll keep it for a time when business lags."

I thought Grandfather was right. If we didn't open a shop or expand the coffeehouse, someone else would; and then it would be too late. Mother always planned for the darkest days. I took a bite of chicken. How much would Watson want for his lot? He spent most of his time in Baltimore. Perhaps Grandfather could inquire discreetly.

Some chicken slid from my fork onto the floor.

"Dash it all," I said.

"Dash it all, dash it all," echoed King George. He swooped down for the treat and flew back to Grandfather's shoulder.

"Matilda, your language," Mother started.

Her lecture was interrupted by a knock at the front door.

"We're not yet open," shouted Grandfather. "Come back in an hour's time."

"A message, Sir," called a boy.

"I'll tend to this matter, Ladies," Grandfather said grandly as he stood. "Don't bestir yourselves."

I ate quickly with one eye on King George. Silas walked under the table, his tail still drooping from his defeat by the squirrel. I tempted him to my lap with his own bite of chicken.

If I could convince Mother to buy an extra urn, it would quickly pay for itself. Then Eliza could cook real dinners, with turtle soup and joints of beef and mutton. If we could get Mr. Jefferson to take his meals here, more business would follow. Maybe even the president himself, and Mrs. Washington for tea.

"Don't feed the cat at the table," said Mother, tugging me back to earth.

"Silas keeps King George away from my plate," I said.

Mother sighed. "I don't know which of you is worse."

Grandfather pulled a coin from his pocket for the messenger. He walked back slowly, rereading the thick sheet of paper in his hand.

"What is that?" asked Mother.

"Nothing, a useless scrap. Nothing of interest for you." A sly smile crept across his face.

"If it's of no importance, then burn it," Mother said. She stacked the dirty plates. "Why are you standing there like an addle-pated nitwit?"

Grandfather looked at the paper again.

"Oh, my," he said with false surprise. "Is that Pernilla Ogilvie's name I see?"

Mother set the pickle dish back on the table. Grandfather continued.

"Pernilla Ogilvie, isn't she the mother of that fine lad you pointed out to me in church? What was it you said—that he'd be a fine match for our Mattie. Yes, that's what it was. But, if you think I should burn it . . ."

Mother dove across the room like a hungry hawk.

"Give that to me," she said, snatching the paper away. She read it hastily. "This is the best news in weeks. Pernilla Ogilvie has invited us to afternoon tea, Matilda."

She read the invitation again.

"Oh, good heavens. She wants us there today!"

"We can't go to tea today," I said. "The shop is too busy. We can't close up or turn away customers. Besides, the Ogilvie girls are snobs. Why would they invite us, except to make fun of our dresses? I'm staying here."

"We would make time for tea at the Ogilvies if they held it at midnight," said Mother. "Be sensible, Matilda. Think of their young Edward."

"I was thinking of their young Edward. That's why I'm not going."

Grandfather stepped between us.

"Matilda," he said in a honey voice. "Of all the maids in our city, surely you deserve a day of rest, a day to drink tea and eat sweet cakes. But if you must stay here, I'm sure your mother and Eliza would be able to find a suitable list of chores to keep you from boredom. You know how they detest idleness."

The kettles, I thought. They'll make me scour the kettles again. My hands ached at the thought.

"And I've heard their cook excels at pastries. Don't give their young Edward a thought. Enjoy yourself. Let your mother enjoy herself. I will direct the replacement troops here at the coffeehouse."

Mother looked at the old man. He just wanted a quiet afternoon, that much was clear. I saw him wink at her. I didn't know which one made me angrier, but somehow they had both won.

"Fine," I said. "We'll go to tea. Huzzah."

As soon as I conceded defeat, Mother turned her attention to the most important issue—tea-drinking clothes. We had tea-buying clothes, tea-brewing clothes, and tea-serving clothes, but we had no taking-tea-with-the-Ogilvies clothes.

Mother's solution lay in the bottom of the trunk in our chamber. She would wear her unfashionable ivory-colored gown, last seen at a victory ball after the War. She said it only had a few stains and fit well. At least she didn't run to fat like some she could name. That was that.

Finding the proper clothes for me was another matter entirely. I could wear my church petticoat, but I needed a proper short gown to cover the bodice. My one fancy short gown was too small, and I hadn't filled out enough to wear any of Mother's castoffs.

"You'll have to wear the old one," she said. "I'll let out the side seams as far as they can go. Perhaps Eliza can do something with your hair."

"You are determined to make this as unpleasant as possible, aren't you?" I asked.

For once, my short-tempered answer did not rile her. "Pretend you're in France, dear," she said lightly. "The ladies there always do their hair."

Eliza's idea of a hairstyle began with brushing me bald. The more I whimpered, the harder she tugged. In the end, I bit my lip and sulked.

"I'll sit nicely at the table," I said. "But you can't force me to talk to their young Edward."

"Hush." Mother stitched my dress as fast as she could, her needle flashing in and out of the fabric like a bumblebee darting through flowers. "It's not too early to search for a suitable man. With your manners, it could take years. Edward Ogilvie has four older brothers. A bride with an established business, like the coffeehouse, is the best he can hope for."

"You make it sound like I'm one of Mrs. Epler's chickens, ready for market. Ow, Eliza, won't you be finished soon?"

"Have patience and keep your head still," she said. "If you cared for your hair properly, I wouldn't have to wrestle it."

Nobody was on my side. I crossed my arms over my chest and pouted. "I don't know which is worse, banishing me to the Ludington farm or marrying me off to an Ogilvie."

Eliza combed through a lock of hair stuck together with dried jam. "You're a few years away from a trip to the altar, Mattie, and you are too soft to live in the country," she said. "You have city hands and a weak back. You wouldn't last a week on the farm."

"Your confidence is overwhelming," I said.

She tugged my hair hard and tied it in a green and gold ribbon. "That's the best I can do," she said. "If we had more time, we could try to curl it."

"No!" I covered my head with my arms. "I like straight hair. And I don't need a husband to run the coffeehouse, Mother. You don't have one."

"Try this on and don't be vulgar," Mother said as she broke the thread with her teeth. "You'll marry one day, don't you worry. Just pray that when you do, your husband won't be fool enough to fall off a ladder and break his neck when he's but five-and-thirty like your father did. The last thing this family needs is another miserable spinster."

Eliza pulled the laces of my stays, cutting off my reply. I gasped and saw tiny black dots.

By the time they had tightened, pinned, and locked me into my clothes, I could feel my stomach rubbing against my backbone. Mother pulled my arms back until my shoulder blades touched, the proper posture for a lady.

"She looks like a china doll," observed Grandfather as we departed.

"I will break just as easily," I muttered.

CHAPTER SEVEN

August 30th, 1793

Wit is the most dangerous talent you can possess. It must be guarded with great discretion and good-nature, otherwise it will create you many enemies.

—John Gregory
A Father's Legacy to his Daughters, 1774

I had to breathe in short puffs as we waited at the front door of the Ogilvie mansion. The stays bit into my stomach and my shift was already sweat-soaked. If this was how the upper class felt all the time, no wonder they were all so cross.

Mother tugged at my bodice to straighten it.

"Try not to look so pained," she said. "We won't stay long. Knowing your grandfather, he'll be giving away the silver on the street corner when we return."

She licked her thumb and wiped a smudge of dirt off my cheek. "You might turn out to be a beauty after all," she said. "You've grown so quickly. I want the best for you."

I looked at her closely, unaccustomed to the gentle tone of her voice. Mother bent down suddenly to brush off the bottom of her gown.

"Look at this dust," she exclaimed. "When I was young, my family had a lovely carriage, and we always rode to tea. We arrived fresh and clean."

She turned around and swatted the hem of my skirt. The door opened and an Ogilvie maid stared at the backside of my grumbling mother.

"Ma'am?" she asked.

Mother stood up hastily.

"Mrs. William Cook Junior and Miss Matilda Cook are here for tea with Mrs. Ogilvie," she told the maid. "The invitation arrived this morning."

The maid showed us into a drawing room as large as the entire first floor of the coffee shop. The long windows were covered with shimmering damask curtains. A crystal chandelier hung over a gleaming mahogany table, around which were clustered a half-dozen Chippendale chairs. Very expensive.

"Lucille, my dear Lucille, how wonderful to see you!" exclaimed Pernilla Ogilvie. She sailed across the room like a man-of-war, showing the brocaded tips of her shoes and layers of lace-trimmed, starched petticoats. Her overpowdered hair left a trail behind her that settled like smoke on the carpet.

Mother's face sagged as she took in Pernilla's gown of gunpowder gray silk, striped with white and blue. Her hand strayed to a stubborn coffee stain just over her hip.

"I'm so glad you could come," Pernilla continued. "I'm about to die from lack of company!"

"Good afternoon, Pernilla. It was very kind of you to invite us. Allow me to present my daughter, Matilda."

I curtsied slightly, conscious of the few threads barely holding me together.

"It's a pleasure to meet you, Ma'am," I said.

"Oh, poor little Matilda. I recall your father well. He was such a handsome man, would have gone far if he had been educated. But it won't do to think about tiresome things today. I declare this has been the worst summer of my life, and I'm counting on you both to lighten my mood."

She squeezed Mother's arm. Mother gritted her teeth.

"I'm parched. Let's have tea and I'll tell you all about this wonderful house that Robert built for me." Mrs. Ogilvie rang a tiny bell on the sideboard. "Girls?"

The Ogilvie daughters, Colette and Jeannine, swept into the room, dressed in matching pink and yellow bombazine gowns, wearing their curled hair piled on top of their heads. I should have let Eliza curl my hair. Dash it all.

Colette was the oldest. Her skin was as pale as clean ice, and dark circles ringed her eyes. Jeannine's head only came up to my shoulder, but she looked sixteen, at least. Her cheeks shone pink and chubby as a baby pig's.

Jeannine whispered something into Colette's ear. Colette closed her eyes briefly, then snapped them open again. I wondered why she was so tired. No doubt exhausted from being waited on hand and foot.

The mothers sat down first, then Colette and Jeannine flopped carelessly onto the Chippendale chairs. I sat carefully so as not to pop any stitches. After two servants brought in silver trays of rolls and bite-sized frosted cakes, Mrs. Ogilvie poured the tea.

"Colette and Jeannine have just finished lessons with their French tutor," Mrs. Ogilvie said. "Are you studying French, Matilda?"

Mother jumped in before I could open my mouth. "You know how old-fashioned my father-in-law is, Pernilla. He prohibits French, no matter how much I implore him. You are so fortunate to have an under-standing husband. Do your sons study French as well?"

"Of course. We've had the French ambassador here to dine any number of times."

While Mrs. Ogilvie recounted what she thought was a hilarious story about "Monsieur L'Ambassadeur," I tried to reach the cake plate. My fingers fell just short. If I stretched all the way across the table, the seam under my arm would split open. Jeannine saw my dilemma, picked up the plate, and passed it in the opposite direc-tion to her mother.

"Why, thank you, dear, how kind," said Mrs. Ogilvie. She chose three cakes and handed the plate to Mother, who took two. As Mother handed the plate to Colette, it tilted and the cakes slid to the floor. A tiny dog with a red ribbon between its ears rushed in and gobbled the fallen cakes. My stomach rumbled.

"So tell me, Lucille, what have you been doing for company this tedious August?" Pernilla asked. "Everyone, simply everyone, has rushed out to their country retreats. It is most annoying."

I struggled to keep a straight face as I pictured Mother amidst the weeds, horseflies, and dead mice in our garden.

Mrs. Ogilvie prattled on.

"President Washington and Martha will soon leave for Virginia, of course, the Nortons and Hepstrudels are in Germantown, and my own sister took her family to New York. Did you know that I planned a gala ball and only two families responded? The rest of society has vanished!"

Jeannine unfolded a silk fan and waved it, blowing a cloud of curls off her forehead. Shielding her mouth from her mother with the fan, she stuck her tongue out at me. Her wretched dog nipped at my shoe under the table.

"The only people left in Philadelphia seem to be shopkeepers and wharf rats. Robert has an appointment with the mayor this very day to insist that he put an end to the rumors of yellow fever."

"I heard a man died of the fever in the middle of the

street, and three black crows flew out of his mouth," said Jeannine.

"Don't be vile, Jeannine," snapped her mother. "Those filthy refugees and creatures who live in the crowded hovels by the river, they're always sick with something. But it is a gross injustice that my gala should suffer because the lower class falls ill. Don't you agree, Lucille?"

Mother struggled to keep the smile on her face as she changed the subject.

"Are your sons still in town, Pernilla?" she asked.

Jeannine's eyebrows went up and her mouth opened. Why did Mother have to be so obvious in her intent? Why not just hang a signboard around my neck: AVAILABLE—FOUL-MOUTHED DAUGHTER?

"All of my brothers are away at school, Mrs. Cook," Jeannine answered quickly. "It's a shame they aren't here to meet you, Matilda. I'm sure you would amuse one of them."

I flinched.

"Colette has recently become engaged to Lord Garthing's son," Jeannine continued. "The gala was to have celebrated the engagement. Have you been courted yet, Matilda?"

"Matilda is a bit young for suitors," interjected Mother. "But I must congratulate you on your good fortune, Colette. When is the wedding to be held?"

Colette dabbed her napkin on her forehead. "Mama, it is rather warm in here."

"Colette always flushes when we discuss the wedding. She is such a delicate creature. Sensitive nerves." Mrs. Ogilvie had icing on the end of her nose.

"Colette tried to avoid our lesson this morning by complaining of a mysterious illness," tattled Jeannine. "She just wants to lie about and read dreadful novels."

"Has any of your sons found a bride?" asked Mother, determined not to let her subject slip away.

Mrs. Ogilvie poured out another cup of tea. "We have many discussions, as you might imagine. My children are a blessing, to be sure, but it requires a great effort to secure the future of each one."

Jeannine picked up the last cake on her plate, slowly bit into it, and licked the icing off her fingers.

"Mother," I said through my teeth. We did not belong here. I did not belong here. Mother may have grown up with carriages and gowns, but I had not. I had to clasp my hands in my lap to keep from slapping Jeannine or shaking the life out of her mangy dog.

Mother ignored me and plowed ahead.

"Has any of your sons shown an interest in business?"

Colette brought her tea cup to her lips, but spilled the tea into her lap. Mrs. Ogilvie didn't notice.

"Trade?" she replied. "Robert thinks that our sons should go into law or banking. Trade is hardly suitable for someone of our background."

Jeannine threw her fan down on the table. "Oh,

Mama, must you be so thick-headed? Mrs. Cook is asking if you might consider Miss Cook as a wife for one of our brothers. And I imagine their filthy little tavern is part of the deal."

I stood so quickly that the seams under my arms ripped open with a snarl. The dog barked shrilly.

"It's not a tavern, it's a coffeehouse!" I said.

"Grog shop," taunted Jeannine.

At that insult my mother rose. A grog shop was where criminals and the other dregs of society gathered to drink whiskey and fight.

"A coffeehouse," Mother explained. "With respectable customers who mind their manners far better than you."

"Oh, girls, ladies," fluttered Mrs. Ogilvie.

Colette grasped the edge of the table and pulled herself to her feet, knocking over the cream pitcher.

"I fear," she said, panting heavily.

We all turned to stare at her.

"Sit down, Colette," said Jeannine.

"I fear," Colette tried again.

"Pernilla, that girl does not look well," said Mother.

"I'm burning," whispered Colette. She crumpled to the flowered carpet in a faint.

While Mrs. Ogilvie shrieked, Mother knelt down and laid the back of her hand against Colette's forehead. "The fever!"

CHAPTER EIGHT

September 2nd, 1793

[I] smelled the breath of death for the first time since all this hardship began, [and] was scared.

—Diary of J. Henry C. Helmuth
Philadelphia, 1793

From the time that Colette Ogilvie collapsed, the church bells of Philadelphia tolled without cease. Guns were fired on the street corners, and a cannon blasted in the public square to purify the air. On top of that, we suffered the constant buzz of mosquitoes, blowflies, and hornets. The din was maddening.

The day after our ill-fated tea party, Mother sent a note to the Ogilvies inquiring about Colette's health, but received no response. They had disappeared. She also sent a note to the Ludingtons. No word from them either, thank heavens.

Many of the wealthy families were fleeing. We were lucky to get four or five customers a day. Mother worried even more than usual, but I was too hot to care. A violent thunderstorm on Sunday cleared the air for a few hours, but when the sun came out Monday, it baked the streets until the rainwater rose in ghostly plumes of steam. I felt like a noodle over-boiled in the stewpot. And the bells continued to toll.

"I'm going to climb the church tower and cut the tongues out of those bells myself," Eliza grumbled as she beat a dozen eggs. "Hand me the nutmeg, child."

I passed her the small grater.

"Don't you have something to do?" she asked. "It's hot enough in here without an extra body breathing on me. What did your mother say before she left?"

"I'm waiting for Grandfather to finish his business in the necessary. He said I could go with him to the newspaper office."

Eliza scowled and waved a towel at the flies buzzing above the bowl. "Pick me some fresh asparagus grass. These pests are a plague."

The bright sun blinded me as I stepped outdoors. The garden looked distressingly poor, even with all the watering I had done and the brief rain. It was a good thing we were able to buy at the market.

The asparagus grass grew along the back fence. I gathered a handful of fronds, cut them at the base, and tied the bunch tightly with a piece of twine. Back in the kitchen, I stood on a chair and hung them from an iron hook in the center ceiling beam.

"There," I said, pushing the chair back against the wall. "That should discourage the flies."

"Thank you. Taste this pudding and tell me if it's right."

I chewed and pondered.

"It needs more sugar."

"You think everything needs more sugar." Eliza wiped the sweat off her face with a handkerchief. "I think that tea with the Ogilvie sisters affected you. Maybe you would be right for their Edward." She stirred the fire and lay on more wood. "Wasn't that long ago folks didn't have any sugar. No coffee or tea, either."

"Please, Eliza, not another history lesson. I'll scream."

Eliza harrumphed and set the pudding over the fire. "Don't know which is worse, you moaning or your mother staring out the window, hoping someone will walk in and lay a shilling on the table. We have ugly days ahead of us. No sugar for anyone, rich or poor, no-no."

I fanned myself with the wooden spoon. "Grandfather says this trouble will soon be over. He says people don't have gumption anymore."

Eliza mumbled something under her breath that I couldn't quite hear. When it came to strong-headed opinions, Eliza, my mother, and my grandfather were evenly matched. She untied her apron and hung it from the hook.

"Where are you going?" I asked. "Grandfather and I could run any errand you need."

"Not this errand, you couldn't." Eliza reached for her pretty straw hat. "The Free African Society is having a meeting about the fever. It should prove a lively gathering. I'll return in time for supper."

Out back, the door of the necessary slammed.

"Mattie Cook!" called Grandfather. "Must I wait all day?"

Andrew Brown's print shop smelled of ink and grease and the sweat of muscular apprentices carrying trays of lead type from the composing table to the printing press. When I was a child, Mr. Brown let me pick out letters and set them in the form. It had been a thrill seeing my words in print.

The printer issued no invitation to me that morning. He was deep in conversation with Mr. Carris as we entered.

"What news, William?" Mr. Brown asked. "Packed your bags for a trip to the country?" He wiped his hands on his apron and sent an apprentice for a bucket of ale.

Grandfather banged his cane on the floor.

"I didn't run from the redcoats, and I won't run from a dockside miasma. What is wrong with people, Andrew? We suffered all kinds of disease in our youth, but folks were sensible. They didn't squall like children and hide in the woods."

Mr. Carris cleared his throat.

"If the yellow fever were a soldier, you'd run it

through with your famous sword and sit down to a hearty dinner. But there may be cause for caution, old friend. Listen to the mayor's orders which Andrew has just printed." He picked up a broadsheet and read:

"ON ADVICE FROM THE COLLEGE OF PHYSICIANS:

1. ALL PERSONS SHOULD AVOID THOSE THAT ARE INFECTED.
2. THE HOMES OF THE SICK SHOULD BE MARKED.
3. SICK PEOPLE SHOULD BE PLACED IN THE CENTER OF LARGE AIRY ROOMS WITHOUT CURTAINS AND SHOULD BE KEPT CLEAN.
4. WE MUST SUPPLY A HOSPITAL FOR THE POOR.
5. ALL BELL TOLLING SHOULD CEASE IMMEDIATELY.
6. THE DEAD SHOULD BE BURIED PRIVATELY.
7. THE STREETS AND WHARVES MUST BE KEPT CLEAN.
8. ALL PERSONS SHOULD AVOID FATIGUE OF THE BODY AND MIND.
9. ALL PERSONS SHOULD AVOID BEING IN THE SUN, DRAFTS, AND EVENING AIR.
10. ALL PERSONS SHOULD DRESS APPROPRIATELY FOR THE WEATHER.
11. ALL PERSONS SHOULD CONSUME ALCOHOL IN MODERATION."

"I'm glad they'll stop ringing the bells," I said.

"Sensible advice, most of it," Grandfather said. "Still, I don't understand why so many run scared."

"They've taken over Rickett's Circus building on Twelfth Street to house the poor," said Mr. Brown.

"Isn't that why we have an almshouse?" asked Grandfather.

"The almshouse is closed. They want to protect their residents from the disease. So the fever victims lie on the floor of Rickett's with little water and no care. Once a day they remove the bodies for burial. A neighbor threatened to burn the place down if the sick are not removed," explained Mr. Carris.

"But where will they go?" asked Grandfather.

"No one knows."

I hadn't heard about that. They were burying fever victims every day?

"How many have died, Mr. Carris?" I asked.

He turned to Mr. Brown.

"How many dead, Andrew?"

Mr. Brown shrugged. "It's hard to say with certainty."

"I've heard several hundred, at least," said Mr. Carris.

Grandfather paused. "Even a few hundred isn't enough to call it an epidemic," he said.

"Some doctors warn we may see a thousand dead before it's over. There are forty-thousand people living in Philadelphia, William. Can you imagine if one in forty were to die?"

The room quieted as we all pondered the number.

"I don't believe it," said Grandfather finally. "People exaggerate. What news from our friend Evans?"

Mr. Brown looked up.

"His wife is ill, and he has closed his shop. My business dwindles daily. I have already lost one of my lads, gone with his family to Wilmington."

"Mrs. Ogilvie said that everyone of fashion has fled to their country estates," I offered.

"I heard one of her daughters was stricken," said Mr. Brown. "Myself, I straddle a fence. One foot stays here in Philadelphia. The other foot is in the country. We know the air there is pure and the people safer. I say safer, mind, not safe. There are reports of fever in Bucks County and Delaware."

"What of the government, then?" Grandfather asked.

"Jefferson still comes into town every morning, though everyone says he'll soon quit and retire to his farm at Monticello," said Mr. Carris.

"Bah! We don't need Jefferson. We have the general. President Washington won't abandon us!"

Mr. Carris blew his nose loudly. "The president retires to Virginia for a respite every September. He is not a man to change his habits. Even if he called the Congress back, few would dare return. I tell you, William, men who stood unafraid before British cannon run in fear from this foul pestilence. I fear for Philadelphia. I fear for the people, I fear for myself."

Grandfather did not say a word as we walked home. I silently counted on my fingers: twenty-eight days until the end of September, then on into October until the first frost. Frost always killed fever. Mr. Carris said it drained the poison from the air. The Ludingtons' were sounding better. Slopping pigs couldn't be that much harder than serving in the front room, and it would be better than falling ill or dying. I'd be there over harvest. They would make me work in the fields and feed me bread and water. But I wouldn't get sick.

Grandfather stayed silent until we approached a limping man dressed in dark rags, pushing a cart.

"Wonder where that fellow's going?" he said. "Looks like he belongs on the waterfront."

A thin white arm flopped over the side of the cart as it jostled over the cobblestones.

"Hullo there, good man!" called Grandfather. "There is no place for the dead up here. Hullo!"

The man ignored us and pressed on steadily.

"Perhaps he is transporting a poor woman to Rickett's Circus, like Mr. Carris said," I suggested.

"She should be moved at night, when good people are safe in their beds. Now what is he doing?"

The man had stopped at the corner of High and Seventh, in front of our coffeehouse.

Grandfather sped up. "Sir, I protest most vehemently!"

I lifted my skirts and ran ahead of Grandfather. An

unnamed fear shot through me. My eyes filled with tears.

"No, this is too much," Grandfather called angrily. "Sir," he shouted. "Take that away from my home. Off with you now and take your cargo, or I should call the constable."

The man turned back and looked at Grandfather, then lifted the handles of the wheelbarrow and dumped the woman on the street.

"Mother!" I screamed.

CHAPTER NINE

September 2nd, 1793

He's the best physician that knows the worthlessness of most medicines.
—Benjamin Franklin
Poor Richard's Almanac, 1733

I stood dumbly while Grandfather knelt by Mother's side.

"She's alive!" he said. "Take her feet, Mattie. We must get her inside."

Eliza screamed as we carried Mother through the front door. She dropped a clay pitcher on the floor. It shattered into bits.

"Is she . . . ?"

"She was overcome by the heat," said Grandfather. "She'll be fine after a short rest. That's all she needs. A short rest."

Mother didn't open her eyes until we tucked her into bed. She looked around in confusion.

"You fainted," Eliza explained.

"It's what you get for working too hard," added Grandfather.

I waited for Mother to throw off the quilt and scold us. Instead, she shivered.

"I'll sleep a few moments, then I'll feel better," she said patting my hand. "Go downstairs, Matilda. Be useful."

Something was desperately wrong. Mother was sleeping in the middle of the day. I wanted to stay and watch over her, but Eliza and Grandfather shooed me out of the room. There was no time to argue; a customer banged through the front door and called for something to drink.

Nothing went right that afternoon. The coffee urn leaked. The biscuits burned in the oven. I dropped an entire drawer of tea leaves on the floor. The gentlemen were all quarrelsome and fractious. I snuck upstairs once, but Mother still slept. Eliza gave me what-for when she caught me.

As I cleared the dirty mugs off the last table, Grandfather stood deep in conversation with Mr. Rowley. I motioned to Eliza.

"Isn't he a doctor?" I asked.

Eliza shook her head.

"Not a proper physician, but he sees sick folk and prescribes medicines. All the real doctors are down on Water Street. It's been a terrible day there. They say bodies are piling up like firewood."

"I don't believe it."

"Shush," said Eliza. "I heard it at the Society. If Reverend Allen said it, you can believe it's the truth. Here they come."

Grandfather introduced Mr. Rowley. I curtsied.

"Mr. Rowley here has vast experience treating female complaints," said Grandfather. "He'll get Lucille back on her pins in no time."

I had my doubts. His hands were uncommonly dirty, and he smelled of rum.

It seemed immodest to let a strange man into our bedchamber, but Grandfather and Eliza showed him in to see the patient. I followed close behind.

He first took Mother's pulse, then felt the skin on her ankles and wrists, then peered down her throat and under her eyelids. He worked without a word, grunting occasionally, and making a tsking sound with his tongue. Mother did not wake. I wanted to throw a bucket of water in her face. It was against the laws of nature for her to lie in bed with the sun so high.

At last Rowley rose from the bed. We waited for him to speak, like a congregation expecting the minister's benediction.

"It is not yellow fever," he said.

Grandfather sighed in relief.

"But Dr. Rush says yellow fever is spreading every-where," Eliza said.

"Dr. Rush likes to alarm people," Mr. Rowley

replied. "There is a great debate about this pestilence. Yesterday a physician I shall not name diagnosed yellow fever in an elderly woman. Her family threw her into the street. She died, but she didn't have yellow fever. It was all a mistake. I use the diagnosis sparingly. And I assure you, there is no fever in this house."

Grandfather beamed.

"See, Matilda? I was right. We have no cause to run out of the city like children scared by a ghost. Lucille will be scolding us by sunrise," he chuckled.

Rowley wagged his finger at Grandfather.

"I wouldn't predict that," he said. "She'll need more than a good nap to recover. Be sure to bathe her every four hours and keep her clean and cool. I'll give some remedies to your servant. And now," he said, holding out his hand and showing his gray teeth, "my fee."

Giving my mother a bath felt upside down and back-side front. I didn't want to do it. Daughters aren't supposed to bathe their mothers, but Eliza could not manage alone.

We moved my bed to Grandfather's chamber and replaced it with the tin bathing tub. Every four hours, we filled the tub with hot water mixed with black pepper and myrrh. The worst part was dragging Mother from her fitful sleep and getting her to sit in the water. The fever had taken hold of her senses, and she wept, calling my father's name.

While Mother dozed in the tub, we stripped the

linen from her bed and laid on fresh. She was supposed to drink dittany tea sweetened with molasses, but it tasted too horrible. As soon as we had her back in bed, Eliza emptied the tub and put more water on to boil.

Mother shivered so hard, her teeth rattled. Even with all the blankets in the house on her, she could not warm. She lay under the faded bedding like a rag doll losing its stuffing, her hair a wild collection of snakes on the pillow, her cornflower blue eyes poisoned with streaks of yellow and red. It hurt to look at her.

After the sun set, Eliza set a candle by her bed.

"You grandfather is sleeping at old man Carris's house," she explained.

"Just as well," I said. "Are you going home?"

"I must," she said. "My brother is expecting me."

I nodded. Eliza lived with her brother's family. They would be very worried if she didn't come home.

"I'll be fine," I said. "I think she'll sleep through the night."

Eliza kissed my forehead. "Don't forget your prayers," she said. "I'll come early and try to bring a doctor with me."

After she left, I locked the doors and closed the shutters. A church bell struck ten times and I shivered. The coffeehouse was filled with shadows and dark noises. I took two extra candles from the clothespress and hurried upstairs to watch over Mother.

She did not notice when I entered the room. Her face was pulled taut in pain, and she jerked in her sleep.

I so wanted to touch her. The tops of her hands were roped with muscle and veins, but her skin was wrinkled and soft. Had she ever enjoyed anything? Had every day been a struggle? Perhaps death would be a release, a rest for the weary.

A slight breeze waltzed through the room. Silas strolled in and jumped onto the bed. He settled himself so gently by her feet that she did not stir. No mice would disturb her, that was understood.

Mother wrinkled her brow and moaned. I smoothed her hair.

"I'm here, Mother," I whispered. "Be still."

She shook her head from side to side on the pillow.

Tears threatened again. I sniffed and tried to control my face. No one could ever tell what Mother thought or felt by looking at her. This was a useful trait. I needed to learn how to do it. There were so many things she had tried to teach me, but I didn't listen. I leaned over to kiss her forehead. A tear slipped out before I could stop it.

I quietly sat beside her and opened my Psalm book, praying for deliverance, or at least the dawn.

I must have dozed off. One moment, the room was still, the next, Mother flew off the pillows and was violently ill, vomiting blood all over the bed and floor. Her eyes rolled back in her head.

I jumped up from the stool.

"Eliza!" I screamed. "Help!"

There was no answer. Eliza was gone. I was alone.

I forced myself back to the bed. Mother panted heavily.

"Everything will be fine," I said as I sponged her face clean. "Just lay still."

Her eyes opened and I smiled at her. Tears pooled in her eyes and spilled down her cheeks. She opened her cracked lips.

"Go . . . away," she whispered. "Leave me."

I recoiled as she leaned over the bed and retched a foul-smelling black fluid onto the floor.

"Oh, stop, please stop," I begged.

"Leave me!" Mother shouted in a ragged voice. "Leave me, go!"

I tried to help her back onto her pillows, but she pushed me away and shook her head.

"Go away!" she repeated.

I ran sobbing to the window. Breathing in the fresh air helped calm my stomach. The houses along the street were shuttered tight and dark. I had to help her. She was depending on me.

"Let me clean you up," I began as I turned away from the window. "You'll feel better in a clean shift. Maybe a bath. Would you like a bath again?"

She was breathing as fast and heavy as a runaway horse. Her hand fumbled along the mucky sheet until it found the small book of Psalms I had dropped.

"I'll put some water on to boil."

Mother threw the book weakly at my head.

"Out," she croaked. "Don't want you sick. Go away!"

CHAPTER TEN

September 6th, 1793

The patient is to be placed in a large empty tub, and two buckets full of water, of the temperature 75 or 80 degrees Fahrenheit's thermometer, . . . are to be thrown on him.
—Dr. Adam Kuhn
Philadelphia, 1793

Eliza shook my shoulder.

I woke at once, with a sharp breath. Outside the sky was turning pale gold. Mockingbirds were singing. Mother slept, her skin the color of an old weathered barn. At least she was alive.

"Your grandfather and I have found help," Eliza whispered. "Dr. Kerr. He's educated, from Scotland."

Dr. Kerr nodded to me. He was a small man wearing a black coat and carrying a small medical case. He set the case on the floor and opened Mother's eyelids with his fingers. She slept on.

"Where's Grandfather?" I asked.

"Waiting downstairs," Eliza said.

"How was she in the night?" Dr. Kerr asked as he started his examination.

"I did everything Mr. Rowley instructed. I bathed her and gave her tea. I tried to keep the bedclothes clean, but . . . we'll wash today. She finally slept after midnight. Do you think she looks better? She feels a little cooler to me. Mr. Rowley said it was just an autumnal fever, nothing serious."

Eliza pulled me close to her. "Shhh," she said gently.

Dr. Kerr rose off the bed. "Damned fool," he growled.

"Excuse me?" I said.

"Rowley, the imposter. Autumnal fever indeed. Your mother has yellow fever. There's no doubt at all."

Yellow fever.

My mouth moved, but I could not breathe. It made no sense. Mother wouldn't allow it. She had given birth to me in the morning and cooked supper for ten that night. She survived the British occupation while my father fought with Washington's troops. Mother would beat back illness with a broom.

A loud moan interrupted my thoughts. Dr. Kerr laid his fingers on Mother's wrist.

"Her pulse is fast and strong," he said. "This is the crisis. She must be bled."

Dear God. "Won't that weaken her more?" I asked.

"Bunkum," Dr. Kerr said angrily. "Dr. Rush has

proven that bleeding is the only way to save a patient this close to the grave."

"But she could mend yet," Eliza said.

Dr. Kerr took a small lancet from his bag. It glinted in the sunlight. He handed me a basin and told Eliza to hold Mother's shoulders. I felt faint.

"Her pulse is full, quick, and tense," he said, pushing up Mother's sleeve. "Hold the basin right against her arm. The pestilence boils within her blood and must be drained."

I flinched as the lancet flashed and blood from Mother's arm poured into the basin. Dr. Kerr handed me a second basin when the first was full. My stomach turned over, but I clenched my jaw and stood firm.

"There," he said finally. He bandaged the cut on her arm and rolled down her sleeve. Mother lay still and silent, but she was breathing. "That was ten ounces of blood. I'll come back tomorrow to take another ten. She needs to purge the disease still in her stomach and bowels. She'll need ten grains of jalap and ten grains of calomel. It will be dirty work to care for her, but it should clean her system efficiently."

"But she's so pale," I said. "Can't the medicines wait a day or so?"

Mother finally roused. She blinked her eyes and pointed at me. "Get her out!" she whispered. "Out!" A cough choked off the rest of her words.

Doctor Kerr and Eliza struggled to calm her.

"Go wait in the kitchen, Mattie," Eliza said. "She

won't settle until you are gone. She doesn't want you here. She's afraid you'll get sick."

Dr. Kerr took me by the arm before I could protest. He led me down the stairs like a lamb on a string.

"She doesn't want you to see the worst. You can help down here. I'm sure Eliza would appreciate a cup of tea. Lucille is a strong woman. With God's mercy she will survive this peril."

Grandfather was waiting for us at the bottom of the stairs.

Dr. Kerr got right to the point. "Yellow fever, William. There's no doubt. I advise you send Matilda out of the city at once."

"What?" I asked.

Grandfather sat heavily in a kitchen chair. "Lucille has been wanting her out of town."

"No!" I stamped my foot on the floor. "You can't send me away! I need to be here—I need to help! You can't send me away."

Dr. Kerr frowned. "I understand, Matilda. These are difficult days for us all. Sensible people have turned mad overnight. They're rinsing their clothes in vinegar and wearing tarred ropes around their necks. This is no place for a young girl like you."

I wiped my eyes on my sleeve. "Why can't Mother come with me? Wouldn't it be better for her in the country air?"

"No town will let her in," explained Dr. Kerr. "They

turn all fever victims away. Your cook can care for your mother. Your grandfather can travel with you. This is the best for all."

Grandfather tried to smile. "We'll make it an adventure, lass." He turned as Eliza came down the steps carrying filthy sheets.

"I've explained to Matilda that she'll be leaving," Dr. Kerr said.

"'Tis best," Eliza said.

"I advise you to hire a wagon as soon as possible," Dr. Kerr said. He picked up his medical case. "They're scarce as hen's teeth. Remember to tie a yellow cloth to the front railing. This coffeehouse is officially closed."

As he closed the door behind him, I started to argue. "We haven't heard from the Ludingtons! I can't turn up without an invitation. Let me stay one more day, Eliza. Grandfather, surely you understand!"

"We want to keep you safe, lass," Grandfather said as he pulled himself to his feet. He paused to cough, then put on his hat. "I'm off to find us a coach."

This could not be happening. They were sending me off, sending me away to strangers!

"You'll let me stay, won't you Eliza?"

Eliza swung the kettle over the fire to boil. "Mattie, you are like kin to me, as is your mother. I can't let you stay here. Lucille doesn't want it and neither do I."

Her face was grim and set in a way I had never seen before. No amount of cajoling would change her mind.

"I'll pack a hamper of food for your trip," she said. She paused by the sideboard to pick something up. "I nearly forgot. This was by the front door when I came in. It's addressed to you."

"Who would send anything to me?"

The parcel was flat and as large as my hand. I fumbled with the brown paper, trying to unwrap it carefully so we could use the paper again.

Eliza looked over my shoulder and made an approving noise, "Um-um-um."

It was a painting, a vase full of delicate flowers, bright blue, lavender, and red carefully painted on a scrap of wood. The flowers looked alive, like they would move if a breeze stirred through the kitchen.

Eliza rummaged through the wrapping paper. "Here," she said. "He sent a note."

Mattie—I write you in haste. Master Peale is closing up the house with his family and assistants inside. To protect us from the fever. We have water from the well and food stored.

My thoughts race. These flowers are for you. Take good care, Mattie. I would not want you sick. We shall watch for balloons again, when this plague has passed.

N.B.

Morning came too quickly and it was time to leave.

"Mattie! The wagon is here!" Eliza called.

It was hard to tell which would collapse first, the

wagon or the horse pulling it. The farmer and his wife sat up front, holding a baby with dried snot across its face. Grandfather rode in the back, waving triumphantly. Eliza eyed the horse with doubt.

"It's a beauty, isn't it?" he bellowed.

The horse stopped in front of the coffeehouse, puffing and wheezing. The farmer jumped down to load my valise and food hamper into the back of the wagon.

Grandfather headed into the house. "Be out in a tic," he promised. He was acting like we were headed for a lark instead of fleeing an epidemic. I shook my head. It wouldn't do to be angry.

I hugged Eliza one last time. She muttered a quiet blessing and tucked a lock of hair into my cap.

"You stay out there until two hard frosts," she warned. "Promise me that."

"Yes, Ma'am," I answered. "Thank you, Eliza. Thank you for everything. You've done so much . . ." I couldn't choke out anything else.

She hugged me tighter.

"Hush, child. I'm doing no more than your mother would do in my place. This is how the Lord wants us to treat each other. She'll be fine and we both know it. Don't worry about her. You take care of yourself."

She turned me around and gave me a shove toward the wagon.

"Thought you said the old man was coming," the farmer said as he tied down the valise.

"Have patience," I said. "Here he comes."

Grandfather stepped onto the porch dressed in his regimental jacket, his sword buckled onto his belt, and King George on his shoulder.

He saluted.

"Captain William Farnsworth Cook, Pennsylvania Fifth Regiment, here to escort you beyond the lines of the dread and terrible enemy, Yellow Fever, Miss Matilda."

He clicked his boots together and offered his arm to me. Eliza laughed as she wiped her eyes with her apron. Grandfather helped me climb up into the wagon before hoisting himself aboard with a grunt. King George circled overhead and squawked. The farmer yelled, "Giyup!" and cracked the whip across the back of the horse.

And so I left home, in a manner quite unpredicted.

CHAPTER ELEVEN

September 7th, 1793

Great numbers of the citizens have shut up
their houses and fled into the country ...
— Letter of Ebenezer Hazard
Philadelphia, 1793

With only one half-starved horse pulling us, it took nearly an hour to be clear of the city line. The dry road was rutted from the wagons and carriages which had fled before us. The insects were vicious. I smacked them on my arms and legs until my skin stung. Grandfather took out his handkerchief and mopped sweat off his face and neck. I waved away a mosquito that buzzed in my ear.

"It's the smell of that baby," I said. "His drawers are full, and it's attracting every bug for miles."

Grandfather chuckled. The laughter caught in his throat and made him cough. I watched with alarm as his face reddened. I pounded his back until he raised his arm in protest.

"I'm fine, child, I'm fine. No need to beat me sense-less."

The farmer turned around in his seat and glared at them.

"He ain't sick, is he? I'll not have fever victims in my wagon."

"Take care you don't drive off the road. We're fine back here. Mind your horse," I snapped.

Grandfather raised an eyebrow.

"You're turning into a regular scold, Mattie Cook. You sound like your mother, ordering menfolk around."

"Some menfolk need ordering."

"That they do." He straightened his legs as best he could between the baskets and clothing bundles. "I propose we enjoy our carriage ride in the country. It would hardly be proper to remove my coat, but if I can beg my lady's indulgence, I will unfasten a button or two." His stiff fingers fumbled with the pewter buttons until they released and he could breathe with ease.

"There," he sighed. "That's better. It's time to review your soldiering lessons."

I groaned. From my crawling days, Grandfather had taught me all the tricks of the American and the British armies, and quite a few from the French. Again and again and again. It would do no good to argue. I was his captive.

"A soldier needs three things to fight," he continued. He held up three fingers and waited for my response.

"One, a sturdy pair of boots," I said. "Two, a full belly. Three, a decent night's sleep."

Grandfather thunked his boots on the floorboards.

"Hey," protested the farmer.

"My boots are sound."

Grandfather belched.

"Tsk, tsk," said the farmer's wife.

"Eliza fed me breakfast enough for two blacksmiths."

He pulled the brim of his hat down over his eyes and settled back against a rolled-up mattress.

"And now I'm going to get some sleep before our coachman delivers us unto the joys of the Ludington family barnyard and their odiferous pigs."

"Pigs," echoed King George.

I settled in alongside him so my head rested on his chest. The rhythmic turning of the wagon wheels, the hum of insects in the barley fields along the road, and the beat of Grandfather's heart blended into a lullaby.

I woke when the wheels stopped turning. I had to shield my eyes from the sun.

"Why are we stopping?" I asked. The farmer didn't answer, but pointed up the road. The baby cried.

Four horsemen armed with muskets blocked our way.

Robbers! I felt for the small purse hidden in my pocket and nudged Grandfather with my elbow. The farmer let his hand drop to the knife handle rising up from his boot. The baby wailed and the horse shifted nervously in his traces. The riders advanced.

One of the men lifted his hat.

"Don't be afraid, we mean you no harm."

The farmer's hand stayed on the knife.

"You are entering Pembroke," said a second man. "Planning on staying here?"

"Just passing through," said the farmer. "I'm taking these folks on up to Gwynedd, and the wife and me are heading for her mother's in Bethlehem."

"We don't have any money," said the farmer's wife.

The first man took a piece of paper from under his coat.

"We aren't highwaymen, Ma'am. We have been authorized by the town council to keep out fever victims. I have to ask you to step down so our doctor here can have a look at you. If you aren't sick, you can pass through town. If you are, you'll have to turn around."

The farmer jumped to the ground. His wife handed their baby down to him, then hopped into the dust herself. I shook Grandfather to wake him. The doctor examined the little family, peering under their eyelids and looking down their throats. I shook Grandfather harder.

"Wake up," I said. "There is a doctor who must see us."

He didn't move. Something twisted inside me. I pinched his nose.

"Grandfather," I said, my voice louder. "Please wake up."

"Is there a problem here, Miss?" The doctor walked to the side of the wagon. He opened one of Grandfather's eyes with his fingers. Grandfather woke with a start.

"What in the name of heaven!" Grandfather shouted. He broke off into a coughing fit. "Water," he croaked.

I looked at the men on horseback.

"Can he have some water, please? We have been traveling in the sun all morning."

The men looked at each other and at the doctor. Grandfather stopped coughing and leaned back wearily.

"I'm fine, child. I can wait until we get to the farm. I seem to have contracted a summer grippe." He tried to sit up straighter. "No need for further delay. Off we go!"

The doctor stepped back and covered his mouth with his hand.

"Take this man back to the city," he commanded. "He is infected with disease."

"No!" the farmer shouted.

One of the horsemen turned his horse and galloped away.

"Nonsense," Grandfather said. "There's nothing wrong. . . ." He broke off coughing again. I stared in horror, first at Grandfather, then at the doctor.

"You must help him," I cried. "If he is sick, you must help him."

The farmer grabbed me under the arms, pulled me from the wagon, and threw me onto the road. He and the doctor lifted Grandfather and deposited him beside me. King George squawked and circled above the commotion.

"They aren't my family," the farmer said as he motioned for his wife to climb aboard. "They only rode in back the last mile or so. They was walking and we picked them up."

"He's lying!" I shouted.

"I don't have no fever," the farmer continued. "My wife and baby are healthy. Let me just drive through so I can get to Bethlehem by nightfall. We won't stop for nothing."

The doctor nodded to the leader of the group.

"Go ahead," the man said. "Make haste."

The farmer brought the whip down with all his strength, and the wagon lurched forward. I stared, mouth open, as the wagon disappeared into a cloud of dust. Our food, our clothing—gone. This couldn't be happening.

"Go back to Philadelphia," the doctor advised. "There are physicians there who will treat you. You can't stay here."

"We can't walk!" I protested. "It's miles!"

"Have you no mercy?" asked Grandfather.

The leader of the group looked down on him.

"We have to take care of our own, Sir."

Grandfather glared at the man. I had never seen him so angry. He looked as if he wanted to run the man through with his sword. But he just stared.

"And I shall look after mine, " Grandfather vowed. "I shall look after mine."

CHAPTER TWELVE

September 8th, 1793

Our inhumane neighbors, instead of sympathizing with us tauntingly proclaim the healthfulness of their own cities ...
—Letter of Ebenezer Hazard
Philadelphia, 1793

We hadn't walked far before Grandfather shook with chills.

"Let's rest a while under that chestnut tree, child," he suggested.

I untied my apron and filled it with timothy grass until it formed a soft pillow for Grandfather's head. I wanted to ask him what we should do next, but he was asleep again before I could say a word.

I bit the inside of my cheek to force back the tears. Crying wouldn't help anything. I put my hand on Grandfather's forehead. It was hot and dripping.

Think, I commanded myself. We have no food or water. We're at least ten miles out of the city. It would take hours to walk back, even if Grandfather felt well. It is just a summer grippe, I told myself. It is just a summer grippe. It had better be a summer grippe, because there is no way to care for him if he is truly ill. I ran my tongue over my dry lips. The first thing we needed was a drink of water.

I slipped Grandfather's canteen from his belt. His chest rose and fell steadily, and his heart thudded regularly.

"I'll be back soon," I whispered as I kissed the damp white hair above his ear.

I walked a few hundred paces south to where the road rose sharply. On top of the hill, I squinted along the horizon until I found what I was looking for.

A line of willow trees.

"Old soldier's trick," I said as I set off. Find a willow tree and you'll soon find water nearby.

The stream was sweet and clear. I drank my fill and washed my face. It was much cooler under the willow than it had been under the chestnut tree. Maybe I could convince Grandfather to move here when he wakes, I thought.

But first I had to find supper. A row of raspberry bushes heavy with ripe fruit lined the other side of the bank. I splashed over and started to pick the fruit.

"Raspberry bushes mean rabbits are about," I told a curious bluebird watching from a milkweed plant.

Grandfather could snare a rabbit, and I'd cook it over

a small fire. With fresh water and food, we could stay under the willow until he regained his strength, then head back to the city. Grandfather would recuperate at home with Mother, and I could care for them both. I ate a handful of berries. My solution was perfect.

"I have a plan," I shouted as I ran back to the chestnut tree. I held my overskirt out in front of me to keep the raspberries from being crushed. The full canteen sloshed against my backside.

Grandfather slowly opened his eyes. I peered closely. His eyes were bloodshot, but they were not yellow. Good, I thought. Just a summer grippe. He pushed himself up to lean against the tree trunk.

"There's my cherub," he said. "I knew you wouldn't leave me to face the enemy alone."

"Here." I fumbled with the canteen. "You need some water. You'll feel much better."

Water spilled along his withered cheeks and down his neck. He wiped his mouth on his sleeve and smiled.

"Better than German wine."

"I have raspberries, too," I said.

"Sit close to me, child," he said. "I want to see your face."

I made myself comfortable in the dirt and shared the berries with him. King George swooped down to help himself to dinner.

"I found a stream of fresh water, like a soldier would, by following the willows. It's beautiful and cool and peaceful. We'll go there after the sun sets. Once you recover your strength, we'll go home and you can rest in your own bed."

Grandfather slowly raised a raspberry to his mouth. A mockingbird in the meadow whistled, and King George took off in pursuit. Cicadas and crickets sang farewell to the sun slipping toward the west.

"I'm a fool," Grandfather said.

"Pardon me?"

"I'm a fool," he repeated. "Worse, an old fool. Lucille was right all along. I should have paid more attention. General Washington used to say my only fault was stubbornness. If not for that . . ."

His voice drifted off but his eyes did not close. Would he be strong enough to walk as far as the willows? Maybe we should try in the morning, after he had a good sleep. We sat in the cooling quiet as the stars crept out from the mantle of night.

"I am concerned for your future," he said. "We must form our battle plans, both for this skirmish and the rest of the war."

I waited for his advice. It did not come. That scared me more than anything. He was waiting for me to decide what to do.

"We'll move camp tomorrow," I finally said.

He nodded. "Whatever you say, Captain."

CHAPTER THIRTEEN

September 10th, 1793

American ladies require a peculiar mode of education.

—Dr. Benjamin Rush
Speech to the Young Ladies Academy
of Philadelphia

The mockingbird whistled and I woke with a start. I laid my hand on Grandfather's chest. His heart beat like a battle drum. My throat was parched, but the canteen was empty. I set off for the stream, King George fluttering behind me. I hoped Grandfather would sleep a while.

"Pretty Mattie, pretty Mattie," the creature called.

"What do you want?" I muttered. How could I get Grandfather to a doctor? If only I could send word to Eliza, she could arrange for a carriage. A carriage with a doctor, and food, and a clean shift.

A breeze rattled through a corn field, lifting the leaves like outstretched arms. King George landed on my shoulder.

"Tea, Mattie! I need tea!"

I brushed him off. "Hush, you foolish creature, or I'll make a pillow out of you."

Mother thought I was safe at Gwynedd, slopping the pigs and hoeing the fields. Would she worry when Grandfather didn't return? I kicked a rock down the road.

Why couldn't I have acted strong and calm like Eliza instead of blubbering like a baby? I disgusted Mother. She knew I was weak. I bet she wanted sons. Instead she got a backward, lazy girl child. I kicked the rock deep into the brambles.

I shook my head to rid it of the dark thoughts. I would only consider the good. Mother was surely getting stronger with every hour. Grandfather and I would find a carriage or wagon that would give us a ride to the Ludingtons'. When we arrived, we would find a letter from Mother telling us that all was well and we could go home. I took a deep breath. It felt better to think about pleasant things.

"Mattie child! Mattie child! Buy me rum!" King George landed on a wild rosebush.

"Go on with you, fleabag. Find us a pot of porridge or an apple pie."

I worked my way around a patch of thistles. The sun burned off the haze, and the dew vanished. My stomach rumbled. If only that blasted farmer had left our food hamper! Along with cinnamon buns, Eliza had packed hotcakes and ham, a crock of cherry preserves, another of garlic pickles, and a hard ball of cheese carefully wrapped.

I reached the stream hungry, hot, and tired. With no prying eyes around, I slipped off one of my petticoats, washed it in the water, and hung it over a willow branch to dry. I waded in up to my knees and stood until my toes felt as if they were in a snowbank. What would Nathaniel think if he saw me like this? Would he think me a finer catch than any trout?

When the cold became unbearable, I climbed out of the water to pick berries. It was hard not to think of our kitchen table with bowls of oyster stew, or corn soup, a platter of duck, sweet potatoes and buttered beans, Indian pudding with molasses—or better yet, apple brown betty with extra sugar on top . . .

The sound of fish leaping from the water interrupted my fantasies. I turned in time to see scales reflecting the sunlight as the fish slid downstream.

Fish! But how to catch one with neither line nor hooks? Where was Nathaniel Benson and his fishing pole when I needed him?

My wet petticoat swayed in the breeze. It would have to do.

I tried to rip open the seam with my teeth, but the tiny stitches that Mother had sewed would not yield. Another fish wiggled to the top of the water to gulp down a water bug.

If I had sewn the skirt, it would have been easy to

tear apart. Instead, I would have to use it whole. I pulled the drawstring at the waist tightly until I could barely poke my thumb through the opening. I would hold open the hem and pray an unusually stupid fish would swim into the trap.

"I bet no soldier ever thought of this one," I said, wading back in the water with my improvised net.

My feet iced right away, and it was hard to find a comfortable position. I had to bend over at the waist, wave the petticoat in the water to make it float, then stand without moving. I wiggled my toes to bring some feeling back in them. How could my feet be so cold while my head was so hot?

A bee buzzed in front of my face. In the distance, I heard a carriage escaping from Philadelphia. Food first, rescue second. I blew the bee away. Where was that stupid parrot? He could be useful and feast on this pest. A fish brushed against my ankle.

"Come little fishy, come down," I murmured. My arms shook from the effort of holding the petticoat open. The fish paused at the edge of the net.

"Just a few more inches. That's it. Keep swimming."

The bee landed on my mob cap just above my eyebrows. I concentrated on the fish.

"You're almost there, my little fried breakfast. Don't stop now."

I prepared to close the petticoat and trap the fish inside.

"One, two . . ."

"Tea, Mattie!"

King George swooped straight at my head and snatched the bee. The explosion of feathers in my face sent me crashing into the water. I came up sputtering and saw the trout flick his tail and head downstream, where there were no girls with petticoats and no parrots.

"I'll roast you!" I shouted at the king, shaking my dripping petticoat in his direction.

"Fresh thing," he replied.

There was no time to try for another fish. Grandfather was alone and without water. I filled the canteen, scoured the bushes for the last berries, and hurried back.

Grandfather's eyes were still clear, but his nose was red and his throat raspy.

"Cold," he said.

"Cold? Are you cold?" How could he be cold? The sun had nearly dried my wet skirts.

He shivered.

"Shall I make a fire?"

He closed his eyes and nodded. Even the effort of speaking a few sentences had exhausted him.

At home, I would borrow a burning twist of paper from a neighbor when all the fires in the house were cold. I couldn't remember the last time I saw a fire started with flint and tinder. I didn't even have flint and tinder.

Grandfather shivered and moaned. I washed his face

and neck with the damp petticoat that didn't catch fish. It seemed to comfort him.

"Is there anything to eat?"

I coughed and shook my head.

"All we have are these berries, Grandfather."

"Of course, I forgot." He ate a few. "We need food."

I thought about telling him how close I had been to capturing that trout, but I hated to admit defeat. Grandfather struggled to remove a pouch from his vest.

"There must be a farm hereabout. Pay for a meal and the loan of a few blankets."

"I can't leave you. You look worse."

He held up his hand. "I'll be fine. I'll sit here and watch the wind blow, think about old friends. We need food and blankets. Off with you."

The sun was at its highest as I set out on my search. It felt like a bonfire spitting embers on my head. I took the first narrow road that branched off toward the east, sure that it would lead to a farm.

The man hoeing a field of potatoes took one look at me and ran off. I followed him to a farmhouse, but the door was locked.

"Go away!" shouted a voice inside. "We have children in here. We can't help you if you have the fever."

What was wrong with the world? Would I next see birds flying backward, or cows crocheting doilies? I walked on, stopping now and then to cough or rest my legs.

The heat rolled to the horizon like waves toward shore. Except for a few raspberries, I had eaten nothing for two days. A flock of geese flew overhead. I could only think of how they would taste with roast potatoes. Grandfather would need more water soon. I needed to go back. I stumbled along, head down, fighting to keep my eyes from closing.

My shoe squashed something brown and green and soft. I shuddered and hurried my pace. I could never abide rotted fruit. It drew flies.

Fruit.

Fruit?

I spun around, wide awake and hungry.

Above me hung gnarled branches heavy with green speckled pears. I grabbed one and bit into it, ignoring the juice that ran down my fingers and chin. I gathered as many pears as I could carry and set off with new energy to find Grandfather. With food, we could hold out for days.

I didn't notice when the pears grew heavy. By the time the chestnut tree was in sight, they felt like tiny anvils weighing me down. I breathed heavily and focused on moving one foot at a time. I turned around. Did I hear voices whispering? A swarm of gnats flew into my eyes. I stumbled and dropped a few pears. I looked up. The chestnut tree seemed farther away. I felt like I was sliding backwards. I wasn't walking on a dirt road, I was slipping across the frozen river. The sun wasn't made of fire, it was a monstrous snowball. My teeth clattered together. What was wrong with me?

I saw a figure stand under the tree. I tried to call Grandfather's name, but could make no sound. The wind carried a roaring sound. Why was I carrying these rocks? I stumbled. Where was Mother? Where was Eliza? The balloon. I'll be up in a minute, Mother. Just let me sleep.

Then, blackness.

CHAPTER FOURTEEN

September 12th-20th, 1793

Hot, dry winds forever blowing,
Dead men to the grave-yards going:
Constant hearses,
Funeral verses;
Oh! what plagues—there is no knowing!
—Philip Freneau
Pestilence: Written During the Prevalence
of a Yellow Fever, 1793

I s she dead?"

"Go away, Barney. She's not ready for you."

"I've got to take the bodies to the pit before I'll get my soup. If she's dead, hand her over. I'm hungry."

I opened my eyes to see who was talking. A large woman holding a candle bent over me, and a man waited in the shadows. The light from the candle burned my eyes. I heard moans on both sides of me, and the sound of hammers and saws in the distance.

Where am I? I thought. I was so cold. Colder than

New Year's Day. I closed my eyes.

"She looks dead," Barney said. His voice faded away.

I slept and the fever fired my dreams with terror. I was back by the chestnut tree. Dust billowed. As I breathed, dirt caked my throat and settled in my lungs. The road was crowded with carriages pulled by wild-eyed horses that crashed into each other as everyone fought to escape.

"What am I supposed to do?" I cried to people rushing by. "I don't know what to do!"

I ran across the meadow and came upon a troop of soldiers marching, with a drummer boy and flag bearer in front.

"Look at me," I called, holding Grandfather's watch. "Tell me what to do."

"*Arrêtez-vous!*" shouted a soldier. "*Arrêtez-vous!*"

"I don't understand you," I said. "I don't speak French." I walked toward the men.

Grandfather appeared by the flag bearer. He wore a bloody shirt. He did not recognize me, and he shouted to his troops.

"Ready," Grandfather drew his sword from the scabbard and held it in the sky. He looked at me and narrowed his angry eyes.

"Aim."

The men aimed their muskets at me. Grandfather slashed the sword through the air.

"Fire!"

"Noooo!"

I jolted awake. Moonlight spilled in through the open windows. I rubbed my eyes, trying to sort out where the nightmare stopped and the waking world began. My sheets and shift were soaked through with sweat, blood, and the foul-smelling black substance that marked a victim of yellow fever.

Yellow fever.

There were beds on either side of me. To my left slept a young woman, her hair in two dirty braids. To my right lay a figure covered with a sheet. A corpse.

Who was dead and who was alive? Was it Grandfather? Was it Mother?

I reached for the sheet, but stopped. My head spun as if I were on a rope swing, twisting dizzily. I closed my eyes until the sensation faded. Taking a deep breath, I lifted the sheet at the side of the body. The hand was thin and the fingers slender, with tapered nails and fine bones. It was not the fleshy, scarred hand of Grandfather. Nor the work-worn hand of my mother. My eyes filled with tears.

Two orderlies walked to the bed of the corpse. They spoke quietly in French. Each man took one end of the dead woman's mattress and lifted, then carried the body away. Just as I slipped back toward sleep, the men brought back the mattress. Empty.

When I woke, the tall windows were shuttered to keep out the sunlight. Steam fairly rose from the reeking bodies of the sick, and sweat dripped off the faces of the nurses and orderlies. The room reminded me of the Ogilvie mansion, only larger. The flowing draperies, expensive carpets, and hand-carved furniture that surely belonged here had been removed. What remained were enormous rooms with high ceilings, and a chandelier that reflected the light like a thousand mirrors.

"Oh, my, now that's looking much better, isn't it? You've beat the Grim Reaper, you have, lassie."

A large woman strode to my bedside. She set a tray on the floor.

"I'm Mrs. Flagg, and I'm here to care for you," she said. "We weren't sure you would make it through the night, but that's past now. It's time for you to eat something, so we can get you home to your loved ones."

Mrs. Flagg helped me sit up. "Your granddad has been waiting this whole time for you. Quite a handsome man, isn't he? A captain in the army, he told me. I'll sneak him in here soon as I get the chance. Now drink this." She held a bowl of beef broth to my lips.

I pushed the bowl away. "How is he? How did we get here?"

She set the bowl on her lap. "He doesn't have yellow fever, if that's what you're asking. Told me his heart was acting up in the heat and he had a bit of a cough, perhaps. But he's such a strong man. Imagine, a man his age carrying someone like you all that distance."

I relaxed. If Grandfather was feeling well enough to

tell exaggerated stories and charm Mrs. Flagg, then there was little to worry about. I reached for the bowl. The salty broth warmed my insides.

"Thank you," I said. "That was delicious."

Mrs. Flagg set the bowl on the floor. She wrung out a rag that had been soaking in soapy water and wiped my face and hands before lifting my dirty hair to wash my neck.

"My mother always said a good wash was the best medicine. If you keep the broth down, we'll let you eat a bit of rice for dinner. Now you rest a spell. I'll be back soon, then the doctor will have a look at you when he makes his rounds. Oh, my gracious! Look who's coming and me wearing this filthy dress."

Grandfather. He never looked so handsome or brave as standing in the middle of the sickroom, his eyes searching all the beds until he found me. I felt like I was six years old again and Grandfather was marching in a parade. He bowed to Mrs. Flagg and sat on the edge of my bed.

"What are you doing in bed, girl? You look healthy enough to jump up and give poor Mrs. Flagg here a hand!" Grandfather said as he kissed my cheek.

Mrs. Flagg wagged her finger at him. "Don't you be giving her any ideas, Captain. What this young thing needs is rest and nourishing food. And she'll get both of them here or my name isn't Bridget Flagg!"

"Bridget," exclaimed Grandfather. "A melodious name for a beautiful lady."

I rolled my eyes while Mrs. Flagg giggled. "Excuse me," I said, interrupting the two of them. "Where are we? And how long have we been here?"

Mrs. Flagg was all business. "No one has told you? Poor little chickie! You're at Bush Hill, and a good thing it is you are!"

Bush Hill!

"We must leave," I said as I pulled the blanket off my legs. "We must go. This is a dangerous place. Grandfather, take me home." I tried to stand, but my legs gave way.

"Now, now, Mattie," Grandfather stammered. Mrs. Flagg took me by the shoulders and sat me back down. Before I knew it, I was lying down with a sheet tucked so tightly over me that I couldn't move.

"That will be enough standing up, young miss," said Mrs. Flagg firmly. "You've nothing to fear. Bush Hill is now a respectable place. Your grandfather was a clever, kind man to bring you here."

The city had turned a mansion on Bush Hill into a hospital for fever victims. According to the gossips, Bush Hill was one step away from Hell, filled with dead bodies and criminals who preyed on the weak. It was a place to stay away from, not a place where a young girl should lay about and sip broth, even if her grandfather was mooning over her nurse.

Mrs. Flagg lifted a mug of cool tea to my mouth. "You listen to me. This here Bush Hill is not the same

Bush Hill of last week. Mr. Stephen Girard, Lord bless his name, has taken over and turned this into a right proper hospital. All them thieving scoundrels have been driven off. You're lucky you were brought here. We have doctors, nurses, medicine, food—everything a fever victim needs. And we have enough problems without you running off the ward."

Grandfather coughed, and I handed him my tea. He emptied the cup and handed it back to me. "Mattie knows all about Stephen Girard," he told Mrs. Flagg. "He has visited our fine establishment several times. Indeed, it has been my honor to break bread with him."

Break bread? Since when did he call stuffing down Eliza's cinnamon rolls in the same room as Stephen Girard (and twenty others) "breaking bread?" Grandfather did admire Mr. Girard, that much was true. Girard was a rich Frenchman with a finger in every pie; he was a merchant, an importer, and a banker. But what did Mr. Girard have to do with Bush Hill?

"He came through here like a hurricane, he did," Mrs. Flagg explained. "He fired the slovenly devils who caused all the trouble. Then he ordered repairs on the water pumps, hired good folks like me, and laid in supplies. We even have a fancy French officer, Dr. Deveze, who supervises the patients, and Mrs. Saville for our matron."

"With a name like Bridget you are surely not French, are you, Mrs. Flagg?" asked Grandfather.

"Good gracious, no, what a question," laughed Mrs. Flagg. "I can barely make out what they're saying half the time, but they work hard, and the pay is good. And I'll tell you this," she said, leaning closer and lowering her voice.

"You'll hear folks say that Dr. Rush is a hero for saving folks with his purges and blood letting. But I've seen different. It's these French doctors here that know how to cure the fever. I don't care if Dr. Rush did sign the Declaration of Independence. I wouldn't let him and his knives near me."

I shivered as I remembered the blood Dr. Kerr had drained from Mother. Maybe Grandfather should return to the house and bring her here. What if Dr. Kerr bled her too much?

"Does Mother know I'm here?" I asked.

Grandfather sat down on my bed. "It's quite a topsy-turvy time we're in, my sweet. We've been gone from home nearly five days now."

"What! Five days!'"

Mrs. Flagg gently pushed me back on the pillow. "Easy, child."

"Much has happened," Grandfather continued. "Once you were installed here, I rode into the city to see Lucille, tell her where you were." He paused to cough. "I found the house locked up tight as you like. Knowing her, she rode out to Ludingtons' to join us. I sent a letter yesterday."

Mrs. Flagg picked up the tray. "There you go. Everything is right with the world. You might not hear back from your mother for a while, though. The post has become most unreliable." She said something else, but I could only hear buzzing. My eyes closed against my will.

"Now look what we've done, Captain," Mrs. Flagg exclaimed. "Here we are chatting like magpies, and your darling granddaughter still so sick."

Grandfather patted my head. "Sleep well, child."

CHAPTER FIFTEEN

September 22nd, 1793

Wives were deserted by husbands, and children by parents. The chambers of diseases were deserted, and the sick left to die of negligence. None could be found to remove the lifeless bodies. Their remains, suffered to decay by piecemeal, filled the air with deadly exhalations, and added tenfold to the devastation.

—Charles Brockden Brown
Arthur Mervyn; or Memoirs of the Year 1793

For long days and nights, stories flew over my head as I slept in my narrow bed at Bush Hill. Nurses and doctors, weeping relatives, and volunteers from the Free African Society whispered their sorrows. They echoed around the beautiful hall with the glittering chandelier.

They told of a small child found huddled around the body of her dead mother. As volunteers placed the mother in a coffin, the child had cried out, "Why are you putting Mamma in that box?" They had to turn the child over to a neighbor and take the mother away for burial.

They told of the dying man who pulled himself to the window of his bedchamber and begged people to bring him a drink of water. Many passed by, hurrying away from the sound of his voice, until a brave soul entered the house to help him.

They told of thieves who crept in and stole jewelry off the dead and dying.

They told of good people who refused to take any money for helping strangers, even though they themselves were poor and near destitute.

They told of the mighty who had fallen ill: Secretary of the Treasury Alexander Hamilton and Dr. Rush himself. Both had recovered, though Dr. Rush's sister had died. Hamilton had fled the city.

They told of terror: patients who had tried to jump out of windows when the fever robbed their reason, screams that pierced the night, people who were buried alive, parents praying to die after burying all their children.

I laid my pillow over my head to protect myself from visions of the dead, but I could not breathe. No one told stories of a painter's assistant named Nathaniel or a cook named Eliza. No one told of my mother. A breeze stirred through the open window, and the crystals of the chandelier struck a gentle chord. The voices faded.

On the tenth morning, I was visited by a French doctor, Dr. Deveze. He did not carry a lancet or bowl. He seemed most concerned with the color of my eyes and tongue, and the temper of my pulse. He grunted with satisfaction.

"She will live," Dr. Deveze said. He turned to Mrs. Flagg. "She stays here one more night, then move her to the barn. You have the hunger?" he asked me.

"Yes," I answered. "I'm famished."

"Feed this girl," he said with a smile. "It is good to see a patient who eats." He patted my hand and moved on.

"Excuse me, excuse me, please," I called after him. What would happen to me? Did we have to walk to Gwynedd? How could we get home? My voice was too weak to carry far, and the doctor was already concentrating on the next jaundiced face.

"What's the trouble, love?" asked Mrs. Flagg as she brought a dinner tray. As I poured out my concerns to her, she tucked a napkin under my chin.

"Too many questions. You'll make yourself sick again. There is only one thing for you to worry about: finishing this here meal. You won't be leaving here for a few days at least. You can't solve tomorrow's problems today, but you can put some meat on those skinny bones."

I nodded and dug into my supper. It didn't take long to finish the small portion of mutton and bread. When it was gone, Mrs. Flagg handed me a bowl of rice and boiled prunes.

"It's got a wee bit of sugar on it," she whispered. "Young ladies need something sweet. And when you're done with that, you'll have a good wash and move to your new bed over in the barn."

The barn wasn't at all what I imagined. The faint smell of manure was everywhere, but the walls were whitewashed and the dirt floor swept clean. The oak doors stood open to let in sunshine and whatever breeze there was. Thick stone walls kept the inside as cool as a cellar. I preferred the smell of hay and horses to the death stench of the hospital. It was a relief to be around people who had the strength to sit up and didn't cry out in pain.

Grandfather looked in on me several times a day. I think he was uncomfortable being around the sick. Mrs. Flagg filled me in on his activities: He helped to organize the delivery of food and the burning of filthy mattresses and rags; he sat in on the committee meetings where decisions were made about raising money and caring for the sick. He had pitched a tent in the yard and told me stories about watching the stars at night. I think he secretly enjoyed the commotion. It reminded him of the War again. It gave him something to do.

I would gladly have joined him, but I was too tired. I spent several days eating mutton that tasted like sawdust, picking bugs off my blanket, and sleeping. I did not have any more nightmares, but I always woke confused, thinking I was surrounded by people I knew, instead of sick strangers. Once I thought I saw Nathaniel, but it was another nameless orderly. I wondered if I were being haunted by ghosts.

How had Nathaniel fared? Was he lying in a sickbed thinking of me? Doubtful. He was probably painting flowers for one of Master Peale's daughters who watched him with stupid cow eyes. I couldn't remember where I had put his painting before we left home. Had I shown it to Mother? What if she found it? Would she burn it?

Thinking of Mother made me twist and turn restlessly. She had not responded to the letters Grandfather sent to the Ludingtons. I could see her ordering the Ludington pigs to march in a straight line, or replanting their corn fields in orderly rows. If I had recovered from the fever, surely she was on her feet again. Unless . . . I couldn't think of that possibility. But why hadn't she written?

Maybe she was glad to be rid of me for a while. Eliza would miss me, but I had no idea how to find her. Some thought that black-skinned people couldn't get yellow fever, but I had seen two sick in the hospital. Eliza lived close to the river, where the disease had started. Who would take care of her if she were sick?

Every day I felt stronger and had more questions. By

the sixth morning, I felt ready to explode with frustration. I left my bed for the first time and walked to the necessary without assistance. This was a sweet victory. After lunch, I was visited by Mrs. Flagg and a frowning clerk with a spotted face who carried an account book, an ink pot, and quill.

"We have not been able to contact your mother, Miss . . . ," said the man as he squinted to read the writing on the page.

"Cook."

"Miss Cook." He scribbled on the page. "You are well enough to leave. It would be immoral to turn a child out into the streets, so you will be taken to the orphan house."

"No! I am not an orphan."

He raised an eyebrow.

"Where is your father?"

"He died years ago."

"Your mother was ill, according to Mrs. Flagg, but you do not know her whereabouts."

"She was sick, but I'm sure she's better now. She's at home, the Cook Coffeehouse. If you will just send me there."

"Other relatives?"

Mrs. Flagg interrupted. "Mattie is the granddaughter of Captain William, the gentleman who has been such a help in the kitchen. I'll fetch him now. He has been waiting for the doctor to release her."

The clerk did not look pleased that I had a living relative. His heart was set on sending me to the orphan house, I could tell. His pen scratched along the page. He blew on it to dry the ink, then closed the book and folded his glasses. He opened his mouth once to say something, but closed it again. He looked like a toad.

Mrs. Flagg returned with Grandfather in tow. His face was bright red and his shirt was stained, but I thought he looked as handsome as ever.

"What's this I hear about you being ready to go back into battle?" Grandfather asked.

The toady clerk answered for me. "Patients who have recovered enough to walk on their own must be discharged, Sir. Provisions can be made to send this child to the orphan house, if you prefer."

I squeaked a protest. "I am not a child!"

"She can stay in the orphan house until her mother is found. If she is found," the clerk amended. "She would be cared for quite well, Sir, I can assure you of that. Life will be difficult for us all until these dark times are over. The orphan house may be the safest place for her."

Grandfather puffed up his chest and crossed his arms. "No kin of mine goes to an orphan house, not as long as I have breath in my body. Your recommendation is insulting, Sir. I served with President Washington himself. I commanded troops that sent redcoats running back across the ocean, and you suggest that I cannot care for this little snippet of a girl? I shall report your impudence to the president."

The man pinched the top of his nose and wrinkled his brow.

"If President Washington is displeased, you may encourage him to come here and speak to me directly," the clerk said. "We have too many lost souls wandering the city streets. I wouldn't want to see this girl join them. But you need not listen to me. My work is done. There is a wagon going into the city tomorrow. You may ride along."

He gave Grandfather the smallest of nods, gathered his supplies, and hopped off.

"Foolish, meddling nitwit," grumbled Grandfather. He would have said more, but just then he broke into a fit of coughing. He pulled at his collar and gasped for air. Mrs. Flagg pushed him down to sit on my bed, and I pounded his back in alarm. When the fit passed, he sat motionless for a moment, then opened his eyes.

"Look at the two of you," he laughed. "What? Did you expect me to expire right here? No such luck. I've got a girl to care for, and," he lifted Mrs. Flagg's hand to his lips, "a lady whom I've promised to take to a ball one day."

Mrs. Flagg dissolved into giggles that reminded me of the Ogilvie sisters.

CHAPTER SIXTEEN

September 24th, 1793

He who sitteth upon the Pale Horse, He whose name is Death, will be sent through the streets of Philadelphia.

—Quaker prophecy
Philadelphia, 1793

Mrs. Flagg blew her nose into her kerchief with a loud honk.

"So much grief packed into one wagon," she said tearfully.

"Fear not, brave Mrs. Flagg," said Grandfather. He saluted her. "Our deepest thanks for your care and shelter. Please accept my most sincere hopes that we may meet again under healthier circumstances."

Mrs. Flagg curtsied deeply. "May the Lord keep and preserve all of you." She waved good-bye, and the wagon rolled forward. Soon Bush Hill faded into the horizon.

Grandfather and I were riding along with five fever

orphans who were being sent to the orphan house. Grandfather rode at the front with the driver, a relatively clean man with neatly combed hair and a smooth face. He quietly whistled a tune, one of Grandfather's favorites. They would be good company for the journey.

I sat on the hardest plank in the back next to a woman named Mrs. Bowles. Two boys huddled together for comfort. They looked like brothers. The other children stared vacantly ahead. One girl looked to be my age. Her neck was dirty and her dress was torn. I wanted to speak to her but couldn't think of what to say. When she saw me looking at her, she turned away.

Mrs. Bowles was a straight-backed woman dressed in Quaker gray. She was older than Mother, with kind eyes and laughter lines that curled around the sides of her mouth. As we drove away from the hospital, she picked up the smallest crying child and sat him in her lap. The child's sobs kept time with the rhythm of horse hooves on the road. He wiped his nose on the front of her dress and snuggled closer in her arms.

"Mrs. Flagg explained that you have been through a great deal," Mrs. Bowles said gently.

"Yes, Ma'am."

"These are trying times. They seem to bring out the best and worst in the people around us." We sat in silence, watching as the slate roofs of the houses on the outskirts of the city came into view. Mosquitoes, gnats, and flies followed the wagon, drawn by the smell of the sweating children and horses. "How old are you, Matilda?"

"Fourteen, fifteen in December."

"And are you feeling recovered from your illness? Fully recovered?!"

I nodded. "My only complaint is that my stomach grumbles all the time."

She smiled and shifted the child in her arms. "That is normal enough for someone your age. If I may inquire?" she began delicately.

"Yes?"

"Have you considered what you might do to help? You have recovered, so you cannot get the fever again. You are young and strong. We have a real need for you."

"How can I help anyone? I'm just a girl." As soon as the words were out of my mouth, I wanted to pinch myself. The first time anyone treats me like a woman and I respond like an infant.

"You are much more than a girl, let me assure you of that. You are older than Susannah there." She inclined her head toward the girl with the dirty neck. "She has lost her family, but we are not taking her in as an orphan. She will help us with the younger children."

The child in Mrs. Bowles's lap stirred and whimpered.

"Shh. Hush," she whispered to the little one. "I know that you have not received any word from your mother yet. It may be better for you to stay with us. We would keep you fed and warm, and you could provide us with a much-needed extra pair of hands."

The wagon had reached the part of the city where new houses and businesses were under construction. Where there should have been an army of carpenters, masons, glaziers, plasterers, and painters, I saw only empty shells of buildings, already falling into disrepair after a few weeks of neglect.

"Grandfather would not allow it," I said with confidence. "If Mother is still out in the country, then we two shall care for each other. He doesn't know the first thing about shopping at the market or cooking, and I need him to chop wood and, and . . . he will make sure I am well."

"It is good you have each other," said Mrs. Bowles in the same placid voice. "But you should not leave your house once you arrive. The streets of Philadelphia are more dangerous than your darkest nightmare. Fever victims lay in the gutters, thieves and wild men lurk on every corner. The markets have little food. You can't wander. If you are determined to return home with your grandfather, then you must stay there until the fever abates."

Grandfather turned to address us. "We may end up at the Ludingtons' farm after all," he said. "Josiah here tells me there's not much food to be found anywhere, Mattie. I'll write to them again as soon as we arrive home."

"Won't do you no good," the driver interrupted. "The post office just closed down. It could take until Christmas before they can deliver letters."

Mrs. Bowles patted my arm. "Don't fret, Matilda. If you like, you may choose to take employment at the orphanage. I'm sure the trustees would approve a small wage if you helped with the cleaning or minding the children. They have for Susannah. She'll help with the laundry."

Susannah didn't look strong enough to wash a teaspoon, much less a tub full of clothing. "What will happen to her when the fever is over?" I whispered.

Mrs. Bowles lowered her voice. "She is at a difficult age. She's too old to be treated as a child, but not old enough to be released on her own. Her parents owned a small house. The trustees will sell that and use the money for her dowry. We will hire her out to work as a servant or scullery maid. She's attractive enough. I'm sure she'll find a husband."

A fly bit the ear of the child on Mrs. Bowles's lap, and his howl cut off the conversation.

Scullery maid, that was one thing I would never be. I imagined Mother's face when she arrived home and found what a splendid job I had done running the coffeehouse. I could just picture it—I would be seeing the last customers out the door when Mother would come up the steps. She would exclaim how clean and well-run the coffeehouse was. Grandfather would point out the fancy dry goods store I was building next door. I would blush, looking quite attractive in my new dress—French, of course. Perhaps I could hire Susannah to do the washing up. That would be a way of helping.

I broke off my daydream to take in our surroundings. Grandfather and the driver had stopped swapping stories. He turned to look back at me anxiously. We were in the center of a dying city.

It was night in the middle of the day. Heat from the brick houses filled the street like a bake oven. Clouds shielded the sun, colors were overshot with gray. No one was about; businesses were closed and houses shuttered. I could hear a woman weeping. Some houses were barred against intruders. Yellow rags fluttered from railings and door knockers—pus yellow, fear yellow—to mark the homes of the sick and the dying. I caught sight of a few men walking, but they fled down alleys at the sound of the wagon.

"What's that?" I asked, pointing to something on the marble steps of a three-story house.

"Don't look, Matilda," said Grandfather. "Turn your head and say a prayer."

I looked. It appeared to be a bundle of bed linens that had been cast out of an upper window, but then I saw a leg and an arm.

"It's a man. Stop the wagon, we must help him!"

"He is past helping, Miss," the driver said as he urged on the horses. "I checked him on the way out to fetch you this morning. He were too far gone to go to the hospital. His family tossed him out so as they wouldn't catch the fever. The death cart will get him soon for burying."

I couldn't help but stare as the wagon rolled by the stoop. He looked about seventeen and wore well-tailored clothes stained with the effects of the fever. Only his polished boots remained clean. His yellow eyes stared lifelessly at the clouds, and flies collected on his open mouth.

"Won't there be a burial, a church service?" I asked as the driver turned east onto Walnut Street.

"Most preachers are sick or too exhausted to rise from their beds. A few stay in the square during the day, that takes care of the praying."

How could the city have changed so much? Yellow fever was wrestling the life out of Philadelphia, infecting the cobblestones, the trees, the nature of the people. Was I living through another nightmare?

"What date is this?" I asked Mrs. Bowles.

"Today is September the twenty-fourth," she answered.

"The twenty-fourth? That's not possible." I counted on my fingers. We fled on the eighth. "When we left, there were reports of a thousand dead. Do you know what the total is now?"

"It's double that at least," she said. "It slowed down those few cool days, but as soon as the temperature rose again, so did the number of corpses."

The driver pulled on his reins to stop the horses. The road was blocked by a line of slow-moving carts, each pushed by a man with a rag tied over his face, each holding a corpse.

"The Potter's Field is ahead," Mrs. Bowles said as she pointed to the front of the line. "That's where they're burying most of the dead. The preachers say a prayer, and someone throws a layer of dirt on top."

Along one side of the square stretched a long row of mounded earth. The grave diggers had dug trenches as deeply as they could, then planted layer after layer of fever victims. Some of the dead were decently sewn into their winding sheets, but most were buried in the clothes they died in.

"A field plowed by the devil," I murmured. "They're not even using coffins."

"I haven't seen a coffin for four, five days now," the driver answered. He flicked the reins and urged the horses on. At Fifth Street, the wagon stopped.

"Here's the orphan house," said Mrs. Bowles. "We've taken over the home of William Ralston, though we'll soon need more room."

It was an ordinary-looking house, more expensive than some, but typical of Philadelphia: brick front, windows trimmed in white paint, metal railings, and a thick oaken door. The driver helped down Mrs. Bowles and Susannah, then each of the children. Mrs. Bowles put Susannah in charge of shepherding three of the children inside, and stayed to wave good-bye. The driver climbed back into his seat, then flicked the reins on the horses' backs.

"Remember what I said, Matilda," she called. "Take care. Whatever you do, take care."

CHAPTER SEVENTEEN

September 24th, 1793

I cannot anticipate nor limit the period, when the devastation and horror too long experienced in this miserable place will have an end.

—Letter of John Walsh, clerk
Philadelphia, 1793

By the time we reached the coffeehouse it was midday. An ugly yellow scrap from a ripped bodice was still tied to the handle of the front door, which was open.

I jumped out of the wagon before it had stopped moving. I leapt up the steps and burst through the doorway.

"Grandfather, hurry!"

The front room was a jumble. Tables and chairs lay helter-skelter. The clock was missing from the mantle; the pewter candleholders were nowhere to be found. King George's bird cage lay on the floor in pieces, as if smashed by a heavy boot. Grandfather hadn't seen the foul-mouthed parrot in days. Had he come home and flown off again?

The destruction in the kitchen was greater. Broken pottery covered the floor. The doors to the pantry stood open, and Eliza's crocks of preserves, the sugar cone, and her spice cabinet were missing. The coffee and tea canisters lay on their sides, empty. The dried meat, beans, and onions that usually hung from the ceiling had vanished. Even the kitchen table was overturned.

Something crunched behind me. I whirled around, but it was only Grandfather picking his way across the broken plates. "What happened here?" he asked quietly. His eyes moved over the mess, but it did not look like he could make sense of it. "I was just here a few days ago. I locked the door, Mattie. I'm sure." His voice was on the edge of trembling.

I picked up pieces of broken glass. "Don't fret," I said. "Someone broke in the window. You locked the door, Grandfather. It's not your fault."

"Did they take anything from upstairs?"

My heart thudded against my stays. Before Grandfather could say another word, I had lifted my skirts and raced up the staircase.

The second floor looked as I had left it, except that Mother was missing. The powerful stench of sickness lingered. I opened the windows and shutters to bring in fresh air, then crossed the hall.

My bed was still in Grandfather's chamber. I glanced

in to make sure everything was in its place. The room still held his presence: his books on the nightstand with an old pipe. A painting of Grandmother hung over his bed, with a picture of the farm where he grew up beside it. Whoever destroyed the first floor hadn't bothered coming up here.

I went downstairs to rejoin Grandfather. The clothespress at the bottom of the stairs was untouched, the bed linens and tablecloths stacked in it as neatly as if Mother had set them there a moment ago. I lingered in front of it. It was almost possible to forget everything if I just focused on the scent of lavender and clean cotton and the beeswax that made the wood glow.

Grandfather was picking through the broken chairs in the front room, trying to salvage something to sit on. I opened all the windows and propped open the doors. There wasn't a breath of air to be had. The room still held the faint smell of coffee and tobacco smoke, but dust coated the furniture and the floor. Spiderwebs hung in the corners of the room. It felt like I had been gone a lifetime.

"Have a seat, girl," Grandfather instructed. "You're still weak."

"Only if you sit as well," I said. "Your face is as red as an overripe cherry." I did not mention how hard he was breathing. We moved two chairs to the door, where the air was a mite cooler. He massaged his left arm.

"Old battle wound," he said when he noticed my

concern. "This arm goes pins and needles from time to time. The heat doesn't help any, nor this commotion."

He was still breathing hard, but his eyes had lost that glazed look they'd had in the kitchen. He needed a good night's sleep in his own bed, I decided.

"Right. When you were here a few days ago, everything was in order and locked up tight. You thought that Mother had gone to the Ludingtons' farm."

"And Eliza," he said. "She would have asked Eliza to join her."

"Eliza wouldn't go. She has family here and would have wanted to help. You know Eliza would never run from trouble."

He nodded his head.

"Whoever came here didn't go abovestairs," I continued. "Maybe they saw the fever rag and thought there was still an invalid in the house."

"It didn't stop them from destroying everything they touched," he said. "Was anything else stolen?"

"Food. They took every scrap of food in the kitchen, even the . . ." I froze. "The strongbox!"

I fumbled with the tread of the hollow stair, then threw it to the side and lifted out the metal box. I opened the lid. It was still there, pence and shillings. Thank heaven for that.

I returned the box to its hiding place. It could be worse, I thought. The house is still standing. We're alive. Mother and Eliza must be somewhere safe, I had to believe that. The fever would soon be over, and our lives would return to normal. I just had to stay clever and strong and find something to eat.

A tear surprised me by rolling down my cheek. "None of that, Mattie girl," I whispered to myself as I scrubbed the tear away. "This is not the time to be childish."

A familiar yowl came from the back door. Silas waited at the threshold, unwilling to risk his paws on the messy floor.

I carried him in to Grandfather. "Here's a friendly face," I said as I held the cat close. "He seems healthy enough." I scratched between his ears. Silas rubbed his face in my hair. "Why didn't you scare those intruders away?"

"They probably fed the beast a bite of ham, and he showed them the way to Eliza's goodies," said Grandfather.

He tried to lift his sword and scabbard to its place over the mantle, but his arms shook too badly. I set Silas down and took the sword from him. "Let me help you," I said. I raised the sword to its resting place.

"Thank you, my sweet," Grandfather said. "Don't know what's come over me."

"I know," I said firmly. "We've just come through a battle and you need time to recuperate." I wagged my finger at him like a commanding officer. "Captain Cook, you must report to your bedroll immediately for an extended leave, Sir. Fresh water will be fetched for you."

He saluted me. "Yes, Ma'am, General Mattie."

I listened with envy as his boots shuffled up the stairs and clumped into his chamber. I wanted to take a nap. Why couldn't someone else come to clean up the mess and fetch the water? Silas looked at me skeptically.

"You're right," I sighed. "If I don't do it, no one will. But first, I need something to eat. Even Mother believed in a good meal before chores. Let's get Grandfather's water and see what we can salvage for supper." Silas followed me outside.

"Oh, my gracious."

The garden looked dead. Insects had devoured most of the leaves and vegetables, leaving behind skeletons of stems and branches. Weeds had exploded between the neat rows. All those weeks of backbreaking work had been for nothing. Hot tears threatened, but my grumbling stomach was more painful.

I drew a bucket of water from the well and used the dipper to drink as much as I could hold. I spilled the dipper over the top of my head, shivering as the cold water trickled down my back. I carried the bucket inside and poured a mug for Grandfather. He was already asleep by the time I entered his room. His color was better, and he was snoring like a barn full of plow horses. I set the mug on the floor and tiptoed back downstairs.

The ground was baked too hard to use the hoe. I

decided to pull up what I could and hope to find something edible overlooked by varmints. A cloud of bugs swarmed around my face every time I touched a withered plant. I weeded the bean patch and found a few hidden string beans for my efforts. The cabbage plants were so infested with worms, I couldn't bring myself to look at them.

Every few minutes, I crawled under the cherry tree for shade and another cool drink of water. Ants covered the cherries that lay on the ground, but I found enough on the tree to settle my stomach. Silas climbed up to a cozy nook between two branches and went to sleep.

"I'll not forget all your help, wretched cat," I muttered as I knelt in the squash patch.

An hour later, I examined my treasure on the kitchen table: two handfuls of green beans, four stunted crookneck squash that had been nibbled by mice, and a few sour cherries. I divided the meal into two piles: one for me, and one for grandfather.

"Not exactly a banquet, is it?" I asked Silas.

Silas jumped on the table and lapped the water in my mug.

"Oh, no, you don't," I said as I lifted Silas off the table. "We still have rules, even if Mother isn't here to enforce them. Cats eat on the floor." I poured a bit of water into what was left of a bowl for him.

I tasted a green bean. Tough as leather, but not as tasty. I suddenly remembered what was missing. I pushed the bean to the side of my mouth and bowed my head.

"Thank you, Father, for keeping me alive. Please punish the terrible people who wrecked our home and stole our food. No, that's not right, they were probably hungry. Punish them a little bit for taking so much. They should have left something behind, and they had no reason to break things. Deal with them as you see fit. Please take care of Mother and Eliza and Grandfather." I sat in silence for a moment. "And Nathaniel."

CHAPTER EIGHTEEN

September 25th, 1793

I think the malady is becoming more alarming, more than one-half [of Philadelphia] has emigrated.

—Letter of John Walsh, clerk
Philadelphia, 1793

Silas woke me the next day by purring next to my head. I rose and stretched, enjoying the coolness brought by the night. Grandfather snored across the room. We had survived one day and one night.

I crept downstairs. I wanted Grandfather to get as much rest as he could. My skin was crusty with filth, and I itched. No doubt I looked a fright and smelled worse. I made my first decision of the day. I needed a bath.

"Much as I hate to start a fire on a day like this, we have to boil water," I told Silas. I fumbled with the flint and tinder until a spark jumped, and I built a respectable blaze. It was a shame there was no one to boast to but Silas.

I didn't bother putting a skirt or bodice over my shift to haul water from the well. It felt too good to walk across the garden unburdened by heavy skirts.

"Nobody can see me," I told Silas, who watched with disapproval. "There isn't another soul for blocks."

I dumped bucket after bucket of water into Eliza's biggest pots and swung them over the fire. As the water heated, I scavenged in the garden again. Gardening at dawn in a thin shift and with loose hair was nearly fun. I felt like a sprite or a hungry leprechaun, turning over leaves in search of a treat, looking under weeds for a pot of gold, or perhaps a turnip. Gardening in nightclothes could become a new fashion, I thought. Imagine plump Mrs. Ogilvie planting radishes in a red-striped nightcap. That would be a sight to turn Philadelphia on its ear!

The bubbling pots of water made the air in the kitchen thick and hard to breathe. I dragged the bathing tub into the front room and filled it with boiling water. When the tub was half full, I added cold water straight from the well until the temperature was comfortable. I closed the shutters, bolted the front door, and closed the door to the kitchen. Assured of privacy, I removed my shift and settled into the warm water.

It felt strange to take a bath like this—the house so quiet, no sound from the street, alone except for a nosy orange cat. I usually bathed once a month, or for special occasions. I stuck my leg up in the air and rubbed it with soap. This felt like a special occasion.

The water soon turned brown with weeks of dirt and sweat. I held my breath and dunked my head under the water. I scrubbed my hair with soap and dunked again, over and over until my hair was free of blood and filth. I rubbed the soap on a rag and scrubbed my skin until it burned. When even the soles of my feet were clean, I dried myself by the kitchen fire.

My skin crawled at the thought of putting on my dirty clothes again. The only other clothes that fit me were someplace in the Pennsylvania countryside with the farmer who had abandoned us. I slipped on my shift and went up to my bedchamber.

I eyed Mother's trunk. I was nearly as tall as she, even if I didn't fill out a bodice the way a grown woman did. I swallowed. "I promise I won't wear any of your clothes to go fishing or climb trees," I said aloud as I opened the latch.

Mother's shift and blue-and-white striped overskirt fit better than I had imagined. They were made of cotton, spun fine and tightly woven, and felt as light as silk after wearing my dirt-encrusted homespun for so long. I twirled around the room, ready for a ball, curtsying to the east corner, and then the west. This would suit me fine.

It was time to wake Grandfather. Too much sleep could be as bad as not enough, and I needed his help in the garden. He was sleeping on his back, his arms thrown to either side. His chest rattled with every breath, and his face was the color of spoiled cream.

Perhaps we should have found a way to stay at Bush Hill. He still wasn't over his cough. Mrs. Flagg would have welcomed the chance to dote on him for a few days. But she had other responsibilities. I could take care of Grandfather.

I shook his shoulder gently. "Grandfather, time to wake. I found a few things to eat, and we have much to do today."

He opened one eye. "I'll have a dozen eggs, a loaf of bread, and basket of plums, please," he mumbled.

"Your stomach will feel better if you don't talk about food," I replied. "But we'll find something today."

I floated down the stairs, clean, fresh, and hungry. Silas trailed behind me, swatting at the edge of my skirt.

"I don't suppose you could be useful and catch me a bite to eat," I said. "No mice, mind you. A fat chicken would be lovely, or a length of sausage, or beef stew . . . Listen to me. I'm as bad as Grandfather!"

I set a small pot of water to boil and added the beans and turnip. The thieves hadn't bothered to take any of the herbs drying overhead. I sprinkled parsley and sweet thyme into the water.

While the soup cooked, I swept the kitchen floor clean of the broken crockery. It made so much noise I did not hear Grandfather enter the room.

"It sounds like you're tearing the house apart board by board," he said. He squinted. "Excuse me, Miss. Have you seen my granddaughter, Mattie? She must be around here somewhere. Filthy little urchin, she is, wearing a grimy dress and a ragged cap."

"Get on with you," I said. "There's no call to be rude, and the bath water is still warm, if you don't mind it gritty."

"I'm a soldier, girl. I've bathed in icy streams."

I interrupted. "Frozen lakes and rushing rivers. I know, a real soldier doesn't need hot water. But I don't want you smelling like a real soldier, thank you very much. Especially in this heat. Once you've finished bathing, put your dirty clothes in the water. I'll wash them later."

Grandfather bathed quickly and was polite about his breakfast soup. It was slightly better than warm water with weeds in it, but not by much.

"Don't suppose there's any way we could convince Eliza to come back right away, is there?" Grandfather asked as he forced himself to swallow another spoonful.

"That wouldn't be right," I said. "I'm sure she's helping the people who are truly needy, folks sick with fever who can't care for themselves. We shouldn't be greedy."

"Is there much food in the garden?" he asked.

"A little," I answered. "We need to find someone who will sell us some bread and meat."

He shook his head slowly. "I don't like the idea of leaving the house," he said. "The world out there has turned upside down." He unbuttoned his top button and coughed. "What if we were gone and Lucille came by with a wagon searching for us? No. We're safe here, and I don't want to hear any more talk of venturing outside, unless it's to the garden. We'll stick to home until we don't have a choice."

I spent the afternoon watering and watering and watering. Grandfather tried to help, but his left arm wouldn't listen to him. As soon as he stepped into the sunshine, his face turned that terrible shade of red again, and he could barely breathe. I begged him to stay on the porch. He blustered and complained at first, but decided it was high time he cleaned and oiled his old rifle. Maybe he could hunt squirrel when the weather cooled.

The pole beans looked better and the squash leaves spread like wide green hands shortly after I watered them. I had never thought a person could be proud of a squash plant, but I was ready to hug all of mine. I hauled buckets of water to the potato patch, drenching the plants which looked healthiest. When the plot was water-soaked, I gently poked the mud with my fingers until I found six fist-sized potatoes. I danced a few steps as I carried my prizes up onto the back porch where Grandfather sat in the shade.

"Potatoes!" I cried. "Potatoes, potatoes, potatoes!"

"What on earth has gotten into you, girl?" he asked.

I spun around his chair. "This is my potato dance, Grandfather. Look what I found. We'll have a real supper tonight. Have you ever seen anything as beautiful as a potato?"

Supper was a royal feast of boiled potatoes seasoned with a scrawny turnip and a few beans. But there was enough to ease the ache in our stomachs. Grandfather found a small bag of roasted coffee beans the thieves had overlooked, and he cooked a pot for us, army style. Hot mud would have tasted better, but he was so pleased with himself, I forced myself to drink it. Oh, for some sugar and cream!

I was ready to fall asleep before the sun set. I carefully pushed the coals to the back of the fireplace and covered them with ashes. I drew a final bucket of water, washed the dishes, and set them on the table. I never did understand why Mother made me dry the dishes. I left them on the table. They would be dry by morning.

After I dumped the wash water at the base of the cherry tree, I dragged up the stairs, ready to fall into bed. Grandfather had already collapsed on his covers, snoring loud enough to shake the stars from the sky. The noise was unbearable. If I stayed, I'd get no sleep at all. I carried my blankets downstairs to the front room and made a soft pallet on the floor.

"If I leave the shutters open, do you promise you won't run off in the night?" I asked Silas.

The cat turned in a circle on the blanket and closed his eyes.

"Very well then. The shutters stay open. We'll both sleep better for it."

I sat next to Silas. It had been a good day, all things

considered. I had managed rather well on my own. I opened Grandfather's Bible. This is what it would be like when I had my own shop, or when I traveled abroad. I would always read before sleeping. One day, I'd be so rich I would have a library full of novels to choose from. But I would always end the evening with a Bible passage.

I turned to Psalm 4:8. "I will both lay me down in peace, and sleep: for thou, Lord, only makest me dwell in safety."

My eyes drooped—enough for one night. I blew out the candle and snuggled on my pillow, asleep before the wick had cooled.

CHAPTER NINETEEN

September 26th, 1793

Shafts of death fly closer and closer to us every day.

—Dr. Benjamin Rush
Letter, 1793

I dreamt of roast beef, sliced pink and dripping with juice. A roast beef bigger than a horse, set on a giant platter that took up the entire front room, surrounded by steaming potatoes and parsnips, and loaves of fresh bread. I had a bowl of butter all to myself, and my very own pitcher of cold apple cider. The smell of mincemeat pie floated in from the kitchen.

I lifted the first bite to my mouth when a noise snapped me awake.

A footstep. A heavy footstep by the window. Silas scrambled off the blanket and ran across the floor.

"What was that?" a strange voice asked.

The room was silent. I held my breath.

"Probably a rat," a second voice answered. "Hurry up, get in there."

Another footstep landed by the window. I turned toward the noise and saw a thin man in the moonlight. He was nearly as tall as the door, but I couldn't see his face. He glanced around the room. His eye did not catch me in the shadows.

A second man entered through the window, shorter than the first.

"There's no one here," the tall one said with more confidence in his voice. "You worry too much."

I closed my eyes. *I am still dreaming,* I thought. These men are not here. I opened my eyes again. The tall one opened one of the cupboards built into the wall by the hearth. The short one peered outside.

"I saw what I saw, and I saw smoke coming out of the chimney today," the short one said. "I don't know why I follow you. We should have gone to Fourth Street. Nobody down there." He tapped the back of a chair nervously.

"You worry too much. Look at this fireplace; there's been no light here for weeks. Come away from that window and help me. They don't serve whiskey here, but they have plenty of pewter, and silver hidden somewhere, no doubt. Check the drawers over there," he said as he pointed to the chest behind me.

My stomach flipped. What should I do? If I screamed, Grandfather might wake, and they could attack us both. The front door was locked and I didn't have the key. I could try to slip out the window and run for help, but who could I run to? Would anyone bother with a trifling robbery when there was death at every door?

The short man took a few steps in my direction, then stopped. He turned his back to me.

"It's too dark over here. I need a candle."

I slipped out of the blankets and into the corner. I needed to get them out of the house. If I could sneak out the window, I might try to scare them off.

The tall one swore.

"You don't need a candle. Shut up and do what you're told."

I froze against the wall as the short one approached, grumbling under his breath. The window was just beyond my left hand, and the chest of drawers was on the other side of the window. The short one stood three feet away. I tried not to breathe.

"Look at this," the short one said as he held up a chess figurine.

Grandfather had won that chess set in a card game with a ship's captain from Siam. He taught me to play chess before I learned how to read. I simmered as the thief rubbed the queen with his dirty fingers.

"It's not worth nothing hereabouts," he said, "but I bet it would fetch a handsome sum in New York." He opened a sack tied to his belt and put the chess piece in.

My hands balled into fists as he collected the rest of

the chess pieces. King, bishop, knight, pawn, all smudged with his fingers, polluted by his breath. How dare he! My jaw tightened. Why were they here, standing in my front room, stealing the hard work of my family? I wanted to drop him into a sack and boot it out the door.

The tall thief lifted Grandfather's sword from the mantle. "Go to New York if you wish, but I know a gentleman in Wilmington who will pay a pretty price for this."

"That's not worth a Continental," the short one laughed. "I could get a better price for my old stockings. Every old man in America drags his rusty sword around and claims he ran it through a hundred British. It's a piece of junk."

I glared at him from my hiding place. Grandfather did kill British soldiers with that sword. He told me so himself. Steady on, Mattie. Crawl out the window as soon as he looks away.

The tall one pulled the sword from the scabbard and slashed it through the air.

"Maybe I won't sell it, then. It could be a handy weapon." He tested the blade with his thumb. "Still sharp, and I don't see a bit of rust. I could become a highwayman." He advanced across the floor toward his partner, waving the sword. "What ho, there, my good man? I have come to relieve you of your purse."

"Give over. Let's fill our bags and leave. You can play at the tavern."

The tall one would not relent. He pressed ahead, continuing to brandish the sword back and forth wildly. The tip of the blade swept by my face. He shuffled forward another foot and waved his arm again, the sword level with my neck.

"No!" I screamed as I ducked. As soon as the sword passed over me, I ran for the kitchen, colliding with the tall man and knocking him down.

"It's a ghost!" the short man cried.

"It's a girl, you fool," the tall one growled as he jumped to his feet. "Get her!"

I ran through the kitchen to the back door and fumbled with the bolt. The thieves' footsteps thudded on the oak floor. Open, open, open!

The bolt slid back. I pushed down the latch and opened the door. I crossed the porch in two steps and ran across the warm earth toward the gate. My foot came down hard on a sharp rock. I cried out, but kept running. The gate was only a few more steps. Faster! Faster!

Two bony hands curled around my shoulders like the claws of a panther and yanked me backward. I hit the ground so hard it knocked the breath out of me. The tall man picked me up and carried me back into the house, where the short man was finishing his search through the chest of drawers.

"You should have let her go," the short one said. "What good is she to us?"

"This haint here will tell us where they've hidden all their silver. I'm sure they have a strongbox as well," the tall man said as he tied my wrists together in front of me.

I spat at him.

Smack! The tall man slapped me across the face, jerking my head backward.

"Don't hit her," the short man protested.

"I'll do what I please," the tall man said as he wiped his face on his sleeve. "Now, missy, the silver and the strongbox. Where are they?"

"We've already been robbed. They took everything. You're too late," I said.

"See? We're too late. Let's go." The short man pulled on his partner's sleeve.

"Shove off," the tall man shouted. "What if she's lying? You think she's going to hand over all her money because we ask her nicely? She needs to be convinced." He drew back his arm to hit me again.

Thump.

"What was that noise?" the tall man demanded.

"What noise?" asked the short man.

"I just heard a noise. Upstairs." He looked at the ceiling.

I shouldn't have screamed. Grandfather must have heard me and gotten out of bed. I needed to get these men out of the house.

"Who's up there? I thought you were alone," said the tall man.

"It's just my cat." I tried to keep the fear from my voice. "Everyone else has died of yellow fever," I lied.

"Saints preserve us, more fever victims," groaned the short man. "Let's go now. This wench is probably fever-poisoned too. She don't look too good."

The tall man hesitated. "She's hiding something," he said. He drew back suddenly and hit me in the face again.

My head rang and lights danced before my eyes.

"Where's the money?" the man demanded. "Tell me where the money is."

"Get away from my granddaughter!"

Grandfather stood in the doorway in his night-shirt, his rifle aimed at the heart of the man who had hit me.

"Oh, Lord," said the short man. He put one leg out the window. "I'm going to Fourth Street. The houses are empty and the cupboards are full."

"He's not going to shoot," said my attacker. "Look at him—he can barely stand. His knees are knocking together. One puff and he'll blow over, isn't that right, old man? Now tell me where you've hidden the money or I'll have to hurt this little girl here."

"I'll count to three," said Grandfather.

He wasn't fooling around. Grandfather never fooled around when he counted to three. The few times he had whipped me had been when he counted to three and I didn't listen.

"One."

The short robber scrambled out the window without another word.

"Two." Grandfather swayed to one side. He was breathing heavily. Too heavily.

"No, Grandfather," I pleaded. "Put the gun down."

He licked his lips and stared down the barrel.

"Three."

Everything happened at once. The gun fired just as the tall man leapt to the side. The blast knocked Grandfather against the door frame. The tall man jumped on Grandfather and punched him in the face. I kicked at the tall man until he hit me with the back of his hand and sent me sprawling.

I struggled to my feet. Grandfather's sword still lay on the floor where the robber had dropped it. I picked up the sword, holding it with two hands. Grandfather had taught me a bit about swordplay along with his other army lessons.

"Let go of him!" I shouted.

The man ignored me. His hands were around Grandfather's throat. Grandfather weakly hit back at the man, but it had no effect. The man struck Grandfather's head against the floor. Grandfather's eyelids fluttered, then closed.

"Nooo!" I screamed. I swung the sword and gashed the thief's shoulder. He howled and rolled to the side, grasping at the bloody wound.

"You cut me," he said in disbelief. "The wench cut me with the sword."

"Get out of my house, before I cut out your heart." I raised the sword and ran at him.

He lurched to the window and crawled through it. I followed, screaming the kinds of words that would have raised every hair on my mother's head. I chased the man for a block before I realized that Grandfather was out of danger. But he needed me back home, not standing in the street in the dead of night brandishing a bloody sword like a pirate.

He was sitting up when I returned.

"Don't move, I'll help you." I dropped the sword to the floor and struggled free of the bonds that held my hands together.

He looked at me with a slow smile. "Always knew you had it in you," he said hoarsely. "You're a fighter, no doubt about that."

"Hush, don't say a word," I cautioned. I grabbed my bedding and made a pillow for his head. "I'll get you some water."

"No," he insisted. He grabbed my shift. "Stay."

The moonlight quivered as thin clouds scuttled across the sky. I could smell the stench of the intruders and the soap Grandfather had used to wash his face before he went to sleep. His eyes started to close, but he forced them open. He fumbled for my hand.

"I'm sorry, Mattie," he panted. "I'm leaving you alone."

I shook my head mutely. No. No. This would not happen. No. Please God. Anything but this.

He nodded once. "My time. Too early. So sorry."

I covered my mouth to hold in the scream and rocked back and forth. After all he had been through, to die like this. Don't die. I couldn't hold the words back. "Don't die, Grandfather. Please don't die. I love you. Please, please. Oh dear God, please don't die."

My face was wet, my tears splashing onto his cheeks.

"Strong," he whispered. "Beautiful. Clever. My sweet Mattie." His eyes closed.

I bent down to kiss his forehead. I thought I heard his last words.

"Love you."

Dead? Grandfather couldn't be dead. My grandfather—candy-giving, wood-chopping, tobacco-smelling grandfather. Who carried me through Philadelphia like a princess. Who knew every politician, printer, carpenter, and captain. Who fed stray dogs. Who curbed Mother's tongue. Who carved me a doll's cradle. Who dried my tears.

Dead.

I held my breath and waited for the earth to stop spinning. The sun need not rise again. There was no reason for the rivers to flow. Birds would never sing.

The sound came straight from my heart, as sharp as the point of a sword. I shrieked to the heavens and pounded the floor with rage. "Nonono! Don't take him! Nonono!"

I picked up the sword and attacked a chair as if it were Death itself. When the chair was a pile of firewood and the sword dull, I fell to my knees by the side of my grandfather's body.

Dead. Growing cold.

I straightened his arms and legs so he might lay with dignity. What should I do next? There was no one to ask. I felt like a baby girl just learning to walk, only the ground under my feet was shaking and I had no one to hold on to.

Silas padded in and rubbed himself along Grandfather's hand. He lay down beside me. I took a shaky breath and looked at the face that had loved me so much. The light was gone from his eyes, blown out. I gently closed his eyelids with my fingertips. I was not afraid to touch him. There were other things to do. Think now. I tried to remember the funerals I'd seen. I dimly remembered seeing an elderly woman's body during a wake when I was younger. There was a bandage round her jaw to keep her mouth closed.

I pulled myself from the floor and marched to the clothespress. I took out a few of our finest napkins and a linen tablecloth. A small package thumped to the floor, but I didn't bother to examine it. I used the napkins to bind up Grandfather's jaw.

I hesitated before moving him onto the tablecloth. Would he want to be buried in his nightshirt? A smile skirted across my face before I could stop it. I thought I heard him chuckle, but his body was as still as ever. He once told me that death is the eternal sleep. What could be more fitting than his nightshirt? Might be more comfortable than forcing him to wear tight clothing for eternity. He'd understand.

I covered him with the tablecloth, but it sent an icy chill through me. I was supposed to cover his face. That's what people would expect. But I couldn't force myself to do it. He had such a kind face. I folded the tablecloth down below his chin. It looked like he was asleep.

An owl hooted outside. I wondered where King George was, if he knew that Grandfather was gone. Maybe that's why King George had left us, to prepare a place for this old soldier. I sniffed and wiped a tear from my face. Silly to cry about a dead parrot, I told myself.

The first tear gave way to another, and then another. I passed the night kneeling by the side of the finest man I had ever known, praying that the morning would not come.

CHAPTER TWENTY

September 27th, 1793

Doctors raving and disputing, death's pale army still recruitin'.

—Philip Freneau
Pestilence: Written During the Prevalence of a Yellow Fever, 1793

Bring out your dead!"

What was that?

"Bring out your dead!" The hoarse voice echoed off the cobblestones and brick houses.

I opened the shutters a crack and peered out. A man dressed in rags pushed a large cart that already contained two corpses—a child and young woman, their skin tinted a pale yellow. The cart was not heavy, but the man walked slowly, as if he were pushing the weight of the world. My hands shook against the window frame. A cold wind from my nightmare blew through my mind. I had to remember something.

"Bring out your dead."

Grandfather. I whirled. His body still lay on the floor. My stomach clenched. I ran outside and threw up what little was in my stomach on the side of the road. It wasn't a nightmare. It truly happened, all of it. The sour taste burned my mouth, and my hands would not stop shaking.

There could be no running from this. Hiding from death was not like hiding from Mother when she wanted me to scrub kettles, or ignoring Silas when he begged for food. I was the only one left.

I had to bury my grandfather, and soon. Hot weather was most unkind to the dead, that was made painfully clear up at Bush Hill. I bit the inside of my cheek to stop the flow of tears. Crying wouldn't help anything. My duty was clear. I understood why the cart man walked so slowly. Death was a heavy companion.

I wiped my mouth on the hem of my dress. The cart turned down Seventh Street and headed south. I ran to catch up with it. A few minutes later, Grandfather's body was loaded into the death cart.

When the man realized I would follow him to the park, he treated Grandfather's body with respect. He gave me time to dash upstairs and find Grandmother's portrait. Grandfather had looked upon her face every night before he fell asleep. I tucked it underneath his arm as he lay in the cart. It pained me that he could not be buried next to her in the churchyard. I hoped that taking her image to the grave with him would be a comfort.

I nodded to the man. He struggled to push the cart. Grandfather's weight made it hard to manage. I tapped him on the shoulder. He looked me up and down once, then moved to the side. I grasped one of the cart handles with both hands. We both heaved, and the wheels rolled. Together we pushed the cart to the burial ground.

The funeral procession for Captain William Farnsworth Cook should have been loud and long, crowded with friends exchanging memories of the grand old man. But the streets were ghosted, colorless and hushed. His casket should have been pulled by a fine white horse, not pushed by a girl and a stranger. I shifted my hands on the heavy handle. A sliver bit into my palm and I couldn't stop the tears.

He was truly gone.

The burial square was quiet, yet busy with activity. Thirty, maybe forty men were methodically digging the earth and laying the dead to rest. Two of them picked up Grandfather's body and laid it on a large canvas cloth that reminded me of a sail. They wrapped the cloth around him and quickly sewed the shroud shut with thick curved needles. I stood behind them, silent and numb. They lifted Grandfather's shroud by the top and the bottom and prepared to fling it into the open grave. My voice erupted.

"Stop!" All heads turned to look at me. I didn't realize what I had done at first. The men set the shroud on the ground.

"You can't just toss him in there like a sack of potatoes," I said. "Where's the minister? You're not supposed to bury people without prayers."

The men looked at each other. The one who stood at Grandfather's feet spoke softly.

"The minister will come by later today and pray for all the dead, Miss. There are so many people alive who need tending to, the dead have to wait their turn. I'm sure God will understand. Now please, Miss, let us get on with this work."

He bent over to pick up the shroud.

"Put him down," I said.

The men ignored me.

A spiteful voice hissed in my head. *Shut up, Mattie*, the voice said. *You're a silly child. You have no business ordering these men around. Stop interfering and get out. This is no place for you. Get your sniveling self to the orphan house where they'll feed you and dry your tears.*

My head throbbed to the rhythm of the shovels biting into the earth. My hands decided what to do without consulting the rest of my body. I shoved the man who spoke to me, shoved him so hard he nearly toppled into the grave. He scrambled to his feet, protesting. I ran up to him and clenched the front of his shirt in my blistered hands.

"This was a great man, Captain William Farnsworth Cook, of the Pennsylvanian Fifth Regiment. He was my grandfather. You will not bury him without a prayer." I spoke slowly, with iron force behind every word.

"The lass is right," said the man who pushed the cart. It was the first time he had spoken. He took a slim book from his pocket and offered it to me. "Can ye read?"

I nodded and took the book from him. It was a copy of the Psalms, the pages worn thin and dirty from frequent use. I stared at the grave diggers. They took off their caps and bowed their heads. Movement in the park stopped, as those watching laid down their shovels and bowed their heads. The book opened to the familiar words. I swallowed, cleared my throat, and began to read loudly, so that all could hear.

"The Lord is my shepherd, I shall not want . . ."

The men around me moved their lips and then gave voice. Our voices rose together as one, proclaiming faith, joining in grief. At the end of the reading, some crossed themselves, others wiped their eyes. I stood straight and tall.

"Thank you."

I handed the book back and walked away. There was nothing more for me to do.

My feet moved, taking me up one street and down the next. I didn't see another person for blocks, not even a grave digger or a physician. The sound of my shoes tapping across the cobblestones echoed down the street like a latecomer sneaking into church. I walked past the homes of people acquainted with my family. They were all deserted. My shift darkened with sweat. Surely I wasn't the only person left in Philadelphia?

My mind whirled. What to do? What to do? I should find a way to the Ludingtons'. No, that would be impossible. I should go to the orphan house; they would take me in. The compass spun wildly. No, I could care for myself. I was not a child. Bush Hill. Mrs. Flagg would see that I was fed, and I could help care for the sick. But the memories of that place were filled with the sound of Grandfather's voice and the rumble of his laugh. Don't borrow trouble, that's what Eliza would say. Don't borrow trouble. I'd go to the market for some food. Then I'd hole up at home and wait for the frost. No one had a duty to me, and I had no claim on anyone else. But it mattered not. I would see my way through.

My stomach took control. The first thing was to find a meal. I felt faint and queasy. I stood in the shade of a linden tree, then set out the short distance to the market.

My steps slowed as I approached the market. No noise greeted me. I checked my bearings twice to make sure I had not taken a wrong turn.

It was empty.

A hot wind blew trash and dirt through the abandoned stalls. It looked like an enormous broom had swept away all the people.

I thought of what Mrs. Bowles had said. Was the fever really keeping the farmers away? But how could city people eat if the market closed? Out of the corner of my eye I saw a dark mass near an overturned basket. It could be potatoes or carrots. I picked up my skirts and hurried over to investigate.

Rats. Shiny, slippery rats, fat and fast, poured in and out of the basket, twitching their noses and flicking their tails. I had never seen rats so far away from the river. Where were the dogs, the cats that kept them away? And what would I do now? How was I going to eat? A chest of gold wouldn't buy any food here today. A coughing fit overtook me and I felt faint. I stumbled into Mrs. Epler's stall and sat in the stray white feathers that littered the ground.

Now what?

Take inventory, check the pack and powder. I was alone; Grandfather was dead and Mother missing. I had survived the fever but still felt weak. There was little food in the garden and no food to buy. Thieves and scoundrels prowled the streets.

My pack was empty and my powder wet. I had no choice but to walk home, where I could at least lock the doors.

When I came upon the open windows of the *Federal Gazette* office, it was a shock. A horse was tethered by the door. I stumbled through the door, eager for a friendly face.

"Can I help you?"

"It's me, Mr. Brown. William Cook's granddaughter."

The printer looked up from his desk. The dark circles under his eyes and lines of worry across his brow made him look as if he had aged years in the course of a month.

"What do you need, Matilda? I've no time for social calls today."

I hesitated. What could Mr. Brown do? I couldn't work a press; he couldn't bring Grandfather back from the grave.

"Please, Sir," I said. "I would like to place an advertisement in your newspaper. I'm searching for my mother. She's gone."

Mr. Brown pulled a stained kerchief out of his trouser pocket and rubbed it over his face and neck.

"Matilda, there is nothing I'd rather do than run an advertisement for your mother. But look about you." He spread his arms to take in the shop. "There is hardly any paper to be had for a hundred miles. The *Gazette* is the last paper being printed in the city, and I have to print on half-sheets. Five other newspapers have closed down. I wish I could flee myself."

He paused and looked out the window. I thought he had forgotten me.

"But I must stay. This paper is the only method of communication left in the city. I must print physicians' notices, orders from the mayor . . ."

His face dropped to his hands. The shop was perfectly quiet, save for the sound of the clock ticking on the wall and a fly caught in a spider's web strung across a grimy windowpane.

"Mr. Brown? Sir?"

He took a deep breath and looked up.

"In the beginning of August, this was the largest city in the United States. Forty thousand people lived here. Near as I can tell," he pointed to the jumble of notes and letters on the desk before him, "more than half the city has fled, twenty thousand people."

"How many dead, Sir?"

"More than three thousand, enough to fill house after house, street after street."

"I went to the market, but found no food," I said.

"Few farmers dare come into town. They charge exorbitant prices for their wares, and get whatever they ask," he said bitterly. "Those who don't die of the fever are beginning to starve. You've seen the rats?"

I nodded.

"The rats thrive. I should write that." He dipped a quill into the ink pot and scribbled a note. "The only creatures to benefit from this pestilence are the rats. Go home, Matilda, take my regards to your grandfather, but tell him he must lock all the doors and pray for frost."

I started to tell him what had happened, but a man burst through the door waving a letter and shouting.

Mr. Brown shooed me from his shop with a wave of his hand. No matter. Telling him wouldn't bring Grandfather back, and it was clear he couldn't help me.

I turned the corner and found myself in front of Warner's hat shop. Mrs. Warner knew my mother a bit. Perhaps they would let me stay a day or two, or share some bread. But the hattery was locked up tight. I couldn't even peek inside through the shutters. No sign of the Warner family.

"Hey there, you! Girlie, by the hatter's!"

A sharp-eyed woman holding a cloth over her face crossed the street. She was older than Mother, with white wisps of hair escaping a dirty mob cap. Her dress was faded. Her eyes narrowed, watching me with suspicion. She stopped a few paces away from me, her cane slightly raised.

"What business do you have here? Off with you!" the woman shouted.

"I mean no harm," I explained. My nose wrinkled at the smell of vinegar coming from the woman. "Do you know where the Warners are?"

The woman stepped backward.

"What is your business here?" she demanded.

"I'm looking for a friend."

The woman considered me for a moment.

"They left for Chester in the dark of night. Warner has kin there. There was horrible screaming and carrying on. The youngest girl fell ill after an apprentice died." She spat the word like a wormy seed. "They threw out the body on the way. And you, do you carry this evil blot on your soul as well?"

"I fell ill, but recovered in the Bush Hill hospital."

"Get back! Stay away from me!" the woman shrieked as she raised her cane higher. "Leave before I call my man. No fever victims here!"

She brought the cane down across my back. The blow sent me face-first into the dirt.

"Leave!" the woman screamed.

I fought my way to my feet before the cane crashed downward again. I ran blindly, ignoring the pain in my throat and the ache in my side. The sun blazed overhead. I lost my way. The cut on my foot started to bleed again. I walked and walked, trying not to remember or feel.

I wandered up one street and down the next. The printer's words haunted me.

Thousands dead.

I saw Grandfather's empty eyes.

No food.

I saw Mother order me to leave her.

No hope.

I passed people weeping in doorways and did not stop. I heard the death carts rattling in the street and did not look up.

A breeze picked up, pushing me eastward, toward the docks, east toward the water, away from the sun. I could see the tops of ships' masts, peeking over the rooftops like trees in the dead of winter. The sodden wharf planks moaned as the tide pulled the river water toward the open sea. My mind floated with dark thoughts.

What did it feel like to die? Was it a peaceful sleep? Some thought it was full of either trumpet-blowing angels or angry devils. Perhaps I was already dead.

I shook my head. Nonsense. Foolish nonsense. I was being weak and foolish. There was no point in wandering like a lost puppy. I needed to get home and sleep. Grandfather would not be proud if he saw me acting so spineless. I needed to captain myself.

My foot scuffed something. I looked down to keep from tripping. A china-faced doll wearing a satin dress lay by the curb, her head shattered, her dress coated with dirt. A few steps away, an abandoned satchel still packed with clean shirts lay open.

I picked up the broken doll and heard a whimpering sound coming from an open doorway. I put my head through the door and waited for my eyes to adjust to the gloom.

A small child cowered in the corner, her blonde hair loose and tangled, her feet bare and black with dirt. She was sucking her thumb and keening to herself. I held out the doll to her. "Is this yours?" I asked.

"Broken," she said.

"Is your mama here? Or your papa? Perhaps they can fix it."

The little girl whispered something. I stepped closer to hear her.

"Mama's broken too," she said.

CHAPTER TWENTY-ONE

September 27th, 1793

*. . . at other places we found a parent dead,
and none but little innocent babes to be seen,
whose ignorance led them to think their
parent was asleep . . .*
—Richard Allen and Absalom Jones
*A Narrative of the Proceedings of the Black
People During the Late Awful Calamity in
Philadelphia in the Year 1793*

Her mother was dead, broken in the eyes of tiny Nell. Her name was the last bit of information I could get from her. Seeing her mother's body, quite clearly a victim of yellow fever, on the bed seemed to make her mute. She stood before me, and before I realized what I had done, I picked her up and cradled her close.

Now what? I couldn't care for Nell; I could barely care for myself. And her mother needed burying, though I didn't relish another trip back to the public square. I had to find someone to care for her.

None of the neighbors who answered their doors knew anything about the family, and they all had enough problems of their own without taking in the child. "You might try Reverend Allen's group," offered one woman. "I seen two women carrying a basket down the alley not long ago. They'll know what to do with the child, and they'll send one to care for the mother."

"Where do I find them?" I asked.

"If you can't find any of their members hereabouts, go down Fifth Street, south of Walnut. They hold meetings there, where they're building a church. You'll find someone there to help, I'll wager."

Fifth Street, south of Walnut. So many blocks to walk, and I'd have to do it with Nell on my hip. But it would be farther to carry her to the orphan house and farther still to the coffeehouse. Nell looked at me. There was no choice. I hoisted her high in my arms and started south.

I kept my eyes open for anyone who might help, but the only folks in the street were sailors, and most of them were drunk. I was nearing the dockside taverns. I held Nell close and tried to walk faster. I did not want to delay in this part of town.

Two black women ahead of me caught the attention of a rowdy group hanging outside a tavern door. They moved swiftly, ignoring the taunts and vicious words the men called after them. I blinked. I rubbed my eyes. There was something about the straight line of the taller woman's back, the color of the cap on her dark head.

"Eliza?" I whispered. I blinked again. The sunlight on the water had left spots dancing in front of my eyes. The women walked steadily away from me, each holding a large basket over their arms.

"Eliza?"

They turned into an alleyway and disappeared.

"Eliza!" I screamed. My feet found their strength, and I took off at a full run, Nell bouncing painfully and gripping my shift for her life. "Eliza!"

A filthy man from the group in front of the tavern broke off from his friends and chased after me.

"Hello, love," he slurred. His breath carried the stench of dockside garbage: whiskey and filth, hardtack and disease. "Come and dance with me."

He tried to pluck Nell from my arms. "Come dance," he insisted.

Nell wound her legs tightly around my waist and bit the man's hand. He howled with outrage while his companions collapsed in laughter. I held tightly to Nell and sprinted for the alley, afraid to look over my shoulder.

"Glad you're on my side," I told Nell. She stuck her thumb back in her mouth as if nothing had happened.

The women were gone. I walked down the alley to a courtyard. It should have been crowded with playing children, chickens and pigs, but was quiet save for the noises made by a tired woman hanging out laundry. I checked behind me. The drunk had found other sport and had not followed us. Nell was grower heavier by the minute. I carried her over to the woman hanging out her wash.

"Please, excuse me, Ma'am. Have you seen two women with baskets walk by here?"

"I seen nobody," the woman answered. "Do you have the fever?"

"No, I'm well."

"You don't look well," the woman said. "You look like a wraith."

"The women, did you see them? They must have passed by. It is most important that I find them."

"Try the Simon house. I heard the door close that-away a moment ago."

"Which one is the Simon house?"

The woman pointed at a house that fronted onto the courtyard, then drew a stained coverlet from the tub at her feet.

I paused in front of the yellow rag tacked to the door. Should I bring Nell in a house with fever victims? She blinked sea green eyes at me. What a foolish question. This child has lived in a fever house for days, weeks maybe. I opened the door and rushed in.

The parlor stood ready for company, with surprisingly fine furniture for the neighborhood, and a portrait on the wall. Thick dust coated the chairs and table, and a man's coat lay on the floor.

I stood unsure of what to do next, when I heard the murmur of voices and footsteps overhead. I gathered up my skirts and went up.

"Eliza?"

A young man leaned over his wife, fanning her face with a paper fan. Two silent children sat on the floor gnawing hard rolls.

"Are you come from the apothecary?" the man asked in a rasping voice.

I shook my head.

"They promised to send Peruvian bark. It may save her yet." He shifted the fan to his other hand. "Why then have you come?"

"I'm looking for Eliza. I was told she was here."

"We have no Eliza here," he answered.

I looked at the children again.

"Did two women just come to deliver those rolls?"

The man nodded. "Saints. Angels. They're from the Free African Society, God bless them. If one is the Eliza you seek, you might find her yet. They had several other homes to visit."

I ran back to the street. Where could she be? I couldn't try each door or go in every house. What if she left one house as I entered another?

There was only one solution.

I set Nell on the ground and cupped my hands around my mouth:

"Eliza!"

I waited until the echo faded among the sounds of the sea gulls high overhead and tried again.

"Eliza!"

"Who calls there?" The faint voice came from an open window.

"Eliza? It's me, Mattie!" I scanned the windows around the courtyard but could not find the face I was looking for. A door closed. There!

Eliza had just reached the bottom step when I slammed into her. She wrapped her arms around me.

"Mattie, Mattie, Mattie," she cooed. "What on earth are you doing here? And where did you find that baby girl?"

CHAPTER TWENTY-TWO

September 27th, 1793

*Yesterday the worst day yet. Even those who
are not sick have eyes tinged with yellow.
More doctors are ill and dying.*
— Dr. Benjamin Rush
Letter, 1793

I t all hit me at once: my fears about Mother; the fever;
Bush Hill; watching Grandfather die; being scared,
alone, and hungry. I cried. I cried a river and poor Eliza
did her best to comfort me. The kinder her words, the
harder I cried.

When I finally paused to catch my breath, she had
one question.

"Why aren't you with your mother at the farm?"

"What do you mean?" I asked. "Mother didn't come
to the farm with us. We never got there."

"Oh, dear," said Eliza. She looked around at the
deepening shadows. "We can't stay here. You are coming
with me to my brother's. You can tell me what happened

as we walk." Eliza pulled her companion aside and spoke quietly. The woman looked at me with an arched eyebrow and walked away.

"Am I taking you away from your work?" I asked. "Do you need to help your friend?"

"It's time for all of us to be safe at home," said Eliza. She pulled a roll from her basket. "Is this little one hungry?"

Nell snatched the roll without a word and took a huge bite.

"That's a good answer," said Eliza. She laid her hand on Nell's forehead and neck.

"I don't think she has the fever," I said. I hesitated. I didn't want Nell to hear me discuss her mother. "She's alone."

Eliza nodded. "We have to hurry," she said. "Do you want me to carry her?"

Nell tensed and locked her arms around my neck. I would have gratefully delivered to her Eliza, but I didn't think my neck would survive. "I'm fine," I lied.

Eliza led me down back streets as I briefly explained what had happened since Grandfather and I left the coffeehouse. I skipped the hardest parts: being alone with Grandfather's body, lying in Bush Hill, the robbers. I didn't want to cry in front of Nell.

Eliza didn't say anything, just shook her head and hurried me along until we reached the narrow street where she lived. Her brother, Joseph, was a cooper. He made barrels, a good trade. Eliza lived with Joseph's family in a small apartment above the cooperage.

I stopped at the bottom of the stairs. I had to know. I covered Nell's ears.

"Where's Mother? She's dead, isn't she? She's dead and you're trying to shield me from it."

Eliza put a hand on her back and stretched. "No, no, she's not dead. Don't think that for a minute. Last I saw her, she was recovered from the fever and bent on following you to the farm."

The knot at the base of my neck loosened. "I must go there, then. I have to find her, Eliza."

"Hush. You can only climb one mountain at a time. Come upstairs and eat some dinner. We'll think better with full bellies. I promise I'll tell you all I know."

She led me up the stairs to a small set of rooms, dimly lit, but clean-smelling and orderly.

"Joseph's wife died last week," Eliza whispered as we paused in the doorway. "He mourns her something terrible. He is still in bed recovering. He's weak, but he'll survive. Thank the Lord the boys haven't taken ill."

Plump-cheeked twins stormed Eliza as soon as she crossed the threshold. "These are the boys." She hugged them tightly before disentangling herself from four arms. "We have company," she said. "This is Mattie, my friend from the coffeehouse. And Mattie's little friend, Nell. Mattie, this is Robert and this is William."

The boys peered shyly at me, then hid their faces in

Eliza's skirts. Nell mimicked them, hiding her face in my neck. If I didn't set her down soon, my arms were going to snap off at the shoulder.

"Is that you, Eliza?" A tiny woman leaning on a cane slowly made her way into the room. Snow-colored hair framed a deeply-lined face the color of aged mahogany. She looked to be the oldest person I had ever seen. The woman walked straight to me and poked my arm.

"Who's this?" she demanded.

As Eliza explained, the old woman harrumphed and snorted.

"So you've got to feed them, too?" she asked.

"No, Ma'am. Eliza doesn't have to feed me," I protested, although that's exactly what I was hoping Eliza would do. "We came across each other in the course of our errands. I'll need to go home soon. And Nell . . ." I wasn't sure how to end that sentence.

The old woman shook her head. "You don't leave until you've eaten. I've seen brooms with more meat on them. The stew is hot, Eliza, and you still have bread and turnips. I'll come again in the morning." She turned in the doorway and pointed a finger twisted with work and age at the boys.

"No trouble from you two. Let your papa sleep and mind Eliza, or I'll send a ghost after you." The boys stared with wide eyes and nodded. The old woman chuckled as she walked out, her cane heavy on the floor. "I'll stop by tomorrow. We'll see if the wagon from

Lititz comes on time. Never thought the day would come when I wished I worked a farm again."

Her voice faded as she made her way down to the street, one slow step at a time. The boys stared at the closed door.

"That was Mother Smith," Eliza told me. "Don't worry, children, she won't send any ghosts. Who wants to help me with Papa's supper?"

The stew in the kettle was made for four, not six. Eliza ladled out a full portion into my bowl, but I poured half of it back.

"I don't need all of this, Eliza. The boys should eat so they don't take sick."

Eliza looked at me closely. "Hmmm," she said. "Could be you're right."

She took a bowl of soup in to her brother Joseph and left me at the table with the children. Nell let me unwind her from my neck when she realized a bowl of soup was for her. She sat on my lap and stared at Robert and William. They slurped up their soup and stared back. I thought they might be close to the same age. A plan began forming in my mind, but I quickly shushed the thought. I didn't have time to dream or plan. I would deal with each hour as it came, one step at a time.

The bustle of the family's evening—clearing away, washing up, getting the boys ready for bed—pushed away all thoughts of the fever for a few hours. Nell fell asleep in my lap shortly after dinner and didn't wake when I laid her on a soft quilt that Eliza spread on the floor. When the boys were finally asleep and Joseph was resting comfortably, Eliza set two chairs by an open window, handed me a mug of lemonade, and motioned for me to sit down.

"Matilda Cook, it is time for the truth. You stay right there on that chair until you tell me what happened—everything."

I never could keep anything from Eliza. The story slid out with all the details: being abandoned on the road, struggling to care for Grandfather, getting the fever. The garden. The intruders. Grandfather's death. Talking about him brought back the tears.

"I did everything wrong, Eliza! I couldn't make a decent meal for Grandfather. I knew he wasn't well, his face was so red. I should have done something—chased the intruders out, or better yet, not been such a baby and left the shutters open just because I was hot. It is all my fault!"

Eliza handed me a clean handkerchief and patted my hand until my sobs quieted.

"Your grandfather was a wise man. You couldn't have saved him, Mattie. It was his time."

I sniffed and took a shaky breath.

"What happened after he died?" she asked.

I filled in the rest of the story quickly, this strange day that began with a burial and ended with a homeless child in my arms.

Eliza watched Nell sleeping. She lay curled on her side, clutching her headless doll. "You understand that she needs to go to the orphan house, don't you? You should probably go there yourself."

My stomach tightened.

"Please, Eliza, don't make me go. I know you think I'm a child, bigger than Nell, but a baby still, and that I need someone to tell me to wash my face and finish my bread." I struggled to control my voice. "I'm not. I'm not a little girl. I can take care of myself."

"We'll talk about it in the morning. We'll talk about everything in the morning." Eliza rubbed her shoulders and stretched her neck.

"Do you feel ill? Do you want to lie down?" I asked.

"I'm just tired and I can't sleep yet. A woman's work is never done, isn't that what the fools say? Here," she pulled a small pair of pants out of a basket at her feet and rummaged for a needle and spool of dark thread. "Robert and William are harder on their clothes than any dock worker I've ever seen. Stitch up the rips while I try to put this shirt back together. I'll tell you what I've been doing."

I bit off a length of thread and slid it through the eye of a needle as Eliza talked.

"A few weeks ago, Dr. Benjamin Rush wrote to Reverend Allen asking for help."

"Reverend Allen from the Free African Society?"

"The same. The doctors thought us Africans couldn't

get yellow fever. Rev. Allen said this was a chance for black people to show we are every bit as good and important and useful as white people. The Society organized folks to visit the sick, to care for them and bury them if they died."

Eliza's voice drifted off as she caught a memory. She took a deep breath and picked her sewing up again.

"Is that why you were visiting those homes this morning?"

Eliza nodded. "Yes. Mother Smith takes my place minding the boys and Joseph. The Society has done a remarkable job, and I don't mind saying that with pride. The Africans of Philadelphia have cared for thousands of people without taking notice of color. If only the doctors had been right, we could look to these days of suffering as days of hope."

I stuck the needle in my thumb.

"What do you mean, 'if only the doctors had been right?'"

Eliza held the shirt up to the light to check the evenness of the stitches.

"After a few weeks of nursing the sick and burying the dead, our own people started to sicken. Black people can get sick with yellow fever just like white people or Indians. I do know some who have never been sick, but there are white people who can say the same thing."

We stitched in silence, each deep in thought.

"Are we going to die, Eliza?" I asked finally.

Eliza snorted.

"That's foolish talk. I'm not going to die. I have too much work to do. Mother Smith there, she won't go until she's ready and the Lord Himself asks for the pleasure of her company. Don't listen to words of despair, Mattie. You must be strong and have faith."

"When will it end?"

"For everything there is a season, remember? When the frost comes, the fever will vanish. We just have to find a way to make it until then."

CHAPTER TWENTY-THREE

September 28th, 1793

There is great distress in the city for want of cash. Friendship is nearly entirely banished from our city.

—Dr. Benjamin Rush
Letter, 1793

Small children can give off powerful smells. Particularly small children who don't know how to wake at night and use the chamber pot.

When I woke on the quilt next to Nell, I smelled her, then realized she was soaking wet. I was merely damp. Eliza shook her head and chuckled. "Babies are the same, no matter what the color. You might as well wash the twins' bedding. They have a similar problem."

There wasn't room in the small apartment to wash, so I scrubbed the quilt and blankets in the courtyard behind the cooperage. Robert, William, and Nell sat on a log and watched me, solemn as three old preachers. By the time the blankets were drying and I had washed the three smelly children, Eliza had gone out to care for the sick and Mother Smith had taken control.

Mother Smith tapped her way around the room with her cane, circling me like a hawk. She made me rewash the breakfast dishes with near boiling water and complained that I left too much dirt behind when I swept. She snorted when she saw my stitching. She cackled out loud when I tried to comb the knots out of Nell's hair.

Too bad my mother never met Mother Smith, I thought as I beat a rug for the third time in the courtyard. They would have gotten along famously, complaining about me and out-scrubbing each other.

She did know how to tell a story, I had to give her that. She sat in Eliza's rocker with the children at her feet and told a tale of magic buckets and flying ships. The children were enchanted. I applied all my force to clean the burned bits from the bottom of the stew pot. Mother Smith hadn't said a word when the stew burned because I forgot to stir it. She didn't have to say a word; the way she lifted her chin as she turned away said everything. I was a complete failure.

When the story was over, the boys trundled off to bed without protest. Nell climbed in my lap and fell asleep sucking her thumb. I worked the knots out of her hair slowly and gently. My stomach rumbled underneath her. I had skipped supper. I figured my portion had been the one which stuck to the bottom of the pot.

Mother Smith pulled her shawl on and prepared to leave.

"Do you think Eliza is all right?" I asked. "Shouldn't she have come home before dark?"

"The pain doesn't go away at sundown," Mother Smith said. "Eliza will stay where she's needed."

Nell stirred and I patted her back.

"Don't love her," warned Mother Smith.

"Pardon me?"

"I said, don't you fall in love with that baby girl. She's not yours. You can't keep her. You had any sense, you'd take her right down to the orphan house tomorrow and hand her over. Don't look back."

"That would be cruel," I said. "She needs some time to get over the shock of, you know"—I mouthed the words "her mother"— "then I'll take her."

Mother Smith shook her head. "You're not doing her any favors. Fact is, you're making it harder on her. She stays with you, you feed her, wash her, sing to her, mother her, then give her away. How's that going to make her feel? You're the cruel one."

Her words dogged me through the night. At first I tried to ignore them. What did Mother Smith know about Nell or me? We were strangers to her. Nell needed someone to hold her. No one at the orphan house would do that; they'd sit her in the corner and scold her.

But Mother Smith was right. I was being selfish, holding Nell close, showing her how to play catch with the twins. I needed her more than she needed me. How long would Eliza keep me, a day maybe, a week if I were lucky? She had her own family to worry about. I needed to do right by Nell and go back to my own home. I had my feet under me now. I knew how to walk.

One good thing about not being able to sleep was that I remembered to wake Nell and have her do her business in the chamber pot. I was just tucking her in long after midnight when Eliza came home. She was too weary to speak.

I rose early and kept the children quiet by serving them breakfast outside. I didn't care if anyone thought it improper. Philadelphia was long past worrying about where children ate their bread, and Eliza needed to sleep. She joined us outside with a cup of tea when she finally woke.

"I don't know when I last slept so much," she said. "Thank you for taking care of the children." She bent over to give Robert and William a kiss. "You seem to have the day well in hand, Miss Mattie." She stopped. Nell was tugging at Eliza's dress. "What do you want, honeybee?"

Nell pointed to her forehead.

"She wants you to kiss her, like you did the boys," I said.

Eliza's laughter sounded clean and strong. She swooped Nell off the ground and gave her a big hug and kiss on the cheek before setting her on the ground to play with the boys. The three of them were chasing a raggy-tailed rooster around the courtyard.

I scuffed a pebble across the street. "That rooster should be in a pen," I said. "He might hurt the children."

"Nonsense," said Eliza. "He won't hurt anything. Why is your face so long?"

I scuffed another pebble. "I need to take Nell to the orphan house. The more I put it off, the harder it will be."

Eliza sat on the stoop. "Mother Smith has been talking to you."

I nodded. "She's right. I know she's right. But it's so hard to think about next week or next month. Look at her. She is happy today. I'm . . . I'm happy today. I don't think we're a burden, are we?"

Eliza shook her head. "But."

"But. I can't just think about today. I have to think ahead. Even if Mother is alive, she won't want another girl child to raise up. She's only just finished with me, and heaven knows that was hard enough. And what if Mother isn't alive?" I raised my hand as Eliza started to speak. "You know it's possible. I've tried to avoid thinking about it, but I can't. In any event, Nell needs to go. I don't want to, but it would be better for her."

The rooster hopped into the air, flapping his wings and sending feathers everywhere. The children shrieked and ran in circles.

Eliza stood up. "If you've made up your mind, then we should leave right now. No telling what the future will bring. I'll get my hat. The boys can stay here with Joseph."

I felt like an turncoat, a traitor. Nell walked between us for a few blocks, then asked me to carry her. She wasn't over losing her mother; that would take a long time, but she seemed content enough to be with me. I knew Eliza's eyes were on me, but she kept her thoughts to herself. I tried to force my thoughts away from the heartbreak. It was impossible. We walked past blocks of empty houses along streets that felt abandoned. I am not abandoning Nell, I told myself sternly; I'm doing the right thing, no matter how much it hurts.

The orphan house appeared much too soon. It looked forbidding, though I knew that was nonsense. It was just a house, a building for unfortunate children. You are doing the right thing, I told myself. It's best for Nell. It's best for Nell.

The woman who answered the door held one screaming infant in her arms and had two crying toddlers grabbing at her skirts. I had to shout to make myself heard above the noise. She bounced up and down, trying to quiet the child in her arms while patting the heads of the others. She looked like a carved whirligig toy with six flying arms and a hopping head.

"I've brought this girl," I began. My throat closed and tears welled up in my eyes. *Don't be such a ninny*, I scolded myself.

"Not another one!" The woman's eyes widened. "Shush, shush, I can't pick you all up at the same time," she said to the crying children, who all needed to blow their noses. She looked at me with desperate eyes. "I'm sorry, that was rude." She shifted the baby to her other shoulder. "Is that the girl?" She motioned toward Nell with her elbow.

I nodded. I still couldn't speak.

"A fever orphan?"

One more nod.

"Is there no one who could take her? This house is just bursting with children right now. Mrs. Bowles, she's in charge here, she's meeting with the mayor's committee right now explaining how we need more space and more money to feed the little ones." One of the children at her feet pushed the other, who exploded into howls. The woman raised her voice to be heard. "I told her the mayor's committee should hold its meeting here. Then they'd give us what we need." She bent down and tried to calm the injured child with her free hand.

I cleared my throat. "You don't have room for more children?"

"This is better than the street," she answered. "But we are very crowded right now, that's the truth. We can't send letters to relatives who might want to help, because the mail isn't being delivered." She bent down and picked up the toddler who was crying the loudest. She had to raise her voice to be heard over the racket. "If you know of anyone who will care for her, then you should take her there. This has become the house of last resort."

Nell looked up at me, her eyes as clear as the sky. She trusted me to do what was right for her. I felt the grip on my heart relax. I looked to Eliza.

"Seems she's better off with you," Eliza noted.

I wanted to dance. "Thank you," I told the harried woman. "Thank you, thank you. Good luck, I mean, best wishes. Good-bye." I dashed down the steps before she could change her mind.

Eliza struggled to catch up with me. "Slow down, slow down. You'll wear yourself out walking that fast in the heat."

I waited for her at the corner. "I did the right thing, didn't I? You saw how crowded it is there. They would never comb her hair or tell her stories. She's better off with me, isn't she?"

Eliza stood with her hands on her hips. "We are all better off together, that's what I think. Let's turn here, the street is shaded."

"The Ogilvies live down here," I said. "Do you think they are still in town?"

"I heard a few stories about them, but I don't know if they're true," Eliza said.

"Tell me, tell me," I begged. "I have to know. Wait. Is it sad? I don't want to know if it's sad."

We stopped in front of the Ogilvie mansion. It was shuttered like the other houses on the street. It seemed like years since Mother and I stood at the front door, waiting for the disastrous tea. I turned Nell loose to pick marigolds from the garden.

"It's a little of both, happy and sad," Eliza said.

I moved Nell away from a rosebush. "Tell me, then. I'll only think about the happy parts."

Eliza joined us by the flower beds. The shade felt like silk on my skin. Bees hummed lazily in the distance and swallows swooped overhead. This was how summer was supposed to feel. I could drink it in all day.

"I don't know if this is true, mind, but I heard this story in the market, just a few days after you'd left with your grandfather. The oldest Ogilvie girl, the one who got sick?"

"Colette. Did she die?"

"Worse."

"What could be worse than dying?"

"You wouldn't think it was worse, but her mamma sure did. Miss Colette came down with an awful case of the fever. You know how they are. They call in this doctor and that doctor. Spend money, fuss and holler. Nothing helps. The girl is burning up. The whole family gathers at her bedside, thinking she's going to Jesus, when she sits up straight in bed and starts screaming for 'Loueey! Loueey!' Turns out this Louis is her husband."

"But wasn't she engaged to Roger Garthing?"

"Um-huh. And listen. This Louis was her French tutor. They had eloped just before she got sick. So everyone starts to scream and carry on, the younger daughter has a temper tantrum cause it turns out she was sweet on this Frenchie too, the mother faints, and their little dog bites the doctor."

One is not supposed to laugh at other people's misfortunes, but I could picture the scene in my mind so perfectly, it caused me to laugh until my sides hurt. "Oh gracious. I shouldn't. Please tell me no one died."

Eliza laughed. "No, they're all alive and making each other miserable. Too spiteful to die, if you ask me. They moved into some relatives' house in Delaware. Poor things—the relatives, I mean. And Louis, the son-in-law, is with them. I heard Miss Colette sat herself in the middle of the street and refused to budge until her mother agreed that he could come with them. Now stir your bones. That's enough storytelling and idling for one day." She peered down the street. "Let's go home."

We decided to stay on the cool street as long as we could. Nell skipped between us, seemingly free of worries and concerns. I was going through all the families I knew, trying to think of someone who might want to take in an adorable imp. Trouble was, I had no way of knowing which families still had parents.

Nell stooped to pick up a daisy on the sidewalk. She held it up to me with a smile, and I tucked it into her hair. We took another step and she found another daisy, laying on the ground, not growing there. As I stood puzzling, three daisies floated through the air. Nell put her hands up to catch them and spun around laughing.

"Eliza, we've had strange weather this summer, but

I've never known daisies to fall from the sky."

We looked up. The houses around us had their shutters closed. . . . Wait. "Look there!" I pointed to a second-story window. The shutters were open a crack, and an unseen hand was pushing out daisies, one by one.

"Well, I never," began Eliza.

"Do you think they need help?" I asked.

"They have the strangest way of showing it," answered Eliza. She went up to the front door and knocked. No one came to the door, though we could both hear people moving within and talking. "I guess they don't want company. Might as well be on our way."

"Wait." I looked up and down the street to get my bearings. "This is the painter's house, Mr. Peale. You know, the one who gave all those strange names to his poor children: Rubens, Raphaelle, Rembrandt, and I don't know what other nonsense."

A daisy fluttered to my feet.

Eliza's eyes widened. "That boy is apprenticed here, isn't he?" she asked. She knew full well the answer.

I looked up at the window. The shutter opened a bit wider and a handful of flowers drifted down. Something fell and crashed inside the house, then the shutter closed quickly.

"We should leave," advised Eliza. "He has a knack for getting in trouble."

I slowly helped Nell gather the flowers. I thought I

saw a shadow move behind an unshuttered downstairs curtain. A tall, lean shadow.

My heart tripped over the thought of Nathaniel Benson, and I smiled in spite of myself. He was alive and still sending me flowers. If I hadn't been carrying Nell, I think I could have skipped all the way back to Eliza's.

There was no more talk of returning me to the coffeehouse or finding a different home for Nell. Joseph and Eliza agreed that I couldn't live alone, not with the deserted streets as dangerous as the crowded sickrooms. We didn't talk about what would happen after the fever. Eliza promised we would find my mother or learn her fate as soon as the epidemic was over. We didn't talk about Nell, we just loved her.

Two days later, Mother Smith sent word that she had to help a family of eight that had just lost their mother.

"Eight? She's going to take care of eight children?" I was stunned.

"If Mother Smith put her mind to it, she could take care of fifty, I've no doubt about that at all," answered Joseph. He was sitting up to the table and making quick work of the fried eggs and corn bread Eliza set before him. His strength was returning along with his appetite.

I took the bread from my plate and broke it into three pieces which I handed to the twins and Nell.

Every day more towns prohibited travel to or from Philadelphia. Even prices higher than any in memory couldn't tempt farmers into the city with fresh food. I tried not to eat more than I absolutely had to. I tightened the drawstring of my skirts a bit more every morning.

"I was going to send the old lady home today if she had turned up," Joseph continued. Robert climbed into his lap. "I'm strong enough to make my way around the house. Mother Smith doesn't have to worry about us no more."

"Do you want Mattie to stay with you?" Eliza asked as she wiped off William's sticky fingers and held out the rag to her brother. Nell held up her hands for me to clean. I brushed them off on my skirt and stood up to clear away the dishes.

"There's little enough business right now," Joseph said as he took the rag to wipe jam off Robert's face. "I think I can control this terrible trio for a bit. Folks out there need all the help they can get, even if it does come from a skinny white girl."

I swallowed hard. Was I really that useless?

Joseph laughed at the expression on my face. "I'm teasing. You worry too much, Mattie. You're a great help."

It was nice to hear him say that.

Robert squirmed away from the rag, but his father caught him and cleaned off most of the mess before he set his son on the floor. Robert raced William into the bedchamber. Nell toddled behind them.

Eliza dusted the crumbs from the table into her hand. "If you don't need her here, then yes, she can be of great help. We need every strong back we can get. She can come with me."

CHAPTER TWENTY-FOUR

October 1st, 1793

We set out to see where we could be useful—
the black people were looked to. We then
offered our services in the public papers, by
advertising that we would remove the dead
and procure nurses.
   —Richard Allen and Absalom Jones
A Narrative of the Proceedings of the Black
People During the Late Awful Calamity in
Philadelphia in the Year 1793

The sights and smells of Eliza's patients were no worse than Bush Hill, but I was not prepared for the heartache. Walking into the homes of strangers, sitting on their furniture, and drying the tears of their children was harder than cleaning up the sick. A dying woman in a cot surrounded by strangers was sorrowful, but a dying woman surrounded by her children, her handiwork, the home where she worked so hard, left me in tears.

We left the house at first light and sometimes did

not return until dark. Joseph kept the children busy in his shop and had supper ready for us when we stumbled home. After a few days of coolness, the sun blazed with heat again, and the air was thick with moisture and infection. The calendar said October, but it felt like July.

Rumors washed over the city. The fever had ended. The fever started again. A shipload of sick people was coming upriver. A cure had been found. No cure was available. An earthquake in the countryside left people saying the end of the world was at hand. The wells had been poisoned. The British were coming. I would have despaired of the hopelessness and confusion. Eliza dismissed the wild tales with a shake of her head.

"They may be true," she said, "but we have work to do. Come now, Mattie."

One boarding house facing the Delaware River had a sick sailor in nearly every room. We went from patient to patient, checking their condition and feeding weak broth to those who had the strength to swallow. The sailors babbled in their own languages, afraid to die on the wrong side of the ocean in a world far away from people who knew their names. The vinegar-soaked cloth tied around my nose could not shield me from the stench of the dying men who baked in the old house.

On our way out, Eliza accepted a basket of dry bread from the woman who ran the boarding house.

"That's nearly the last of the flour," the woman said. "It'll be sawdust after this, just like the War."

"Sawdust?" I asked. "You can make bread?"

"It will have some flour in it," Eliza said as she thanked the woman, "but the sawdust will stretch the wheat, make it go farther. When your stomach hurts enough, the tongue won't mind the taste."

At Barrett's apothecary, Eliza purchased jalap and Bohea tea. I walked around the shop while Eliza argued with the owner about his prices. Grandfather used to bring me to Barrett's to buy soft-shell almonds and figs from the big barrel. This was the kind of shop I had always dreamed of. Back then the shelves had been crowded with colored glass jars, wooden boxes, casks, and bags, all labeled with the spidery handwriting of Mr. Barrett. Now they were covered with dust and the shells of dead insects.

Eliza finished her purchases, grabbed my hand, and slammed the door behind us.

"He's a scurrilous dog, that man," she muttered.

"Why do you say that? He seemed friendly enough. And he has the medicine you needed."

"The price of jalap and tea has climbed to the clouds since the fever struck. If he really cared, he would charge a decent price instead of robbing the sick. Pharmacists and coffin makers are the only people who profit from this plague."

"Don't forget the thieves," I added.

Eliza made a noise in her throat and squinted at the house numbers.

"We are going to number thirty. The Sharp family. They could have left for the country long ago, but he's a merchant and didn't want to leave the business. Then a serving girl came down with the fever and Sharp's wife wouldn't abandon the girl, bless her."

"What happened?"

"The serving girl recovered, but Mr. Sharp died. His mind went before the end, and he raged throughout the house like a mad bull, destroying all he touched. Mrs. Sharp suffered a mild case but is back on her feet again. She fears for her son and daughter, they are both ill in bed. Here it is."

Eliza headed straight for the stairs that led to the bedchambers overhead, but I stopped in the front hall to stare. The furniture lay in heaps of splintered wood and feathers. A looking glass had been dashed to thousands of pieces, and the gilt frame torn apart. The curtains were torn from the windows, and a door was nearly ripped off its hinges. Mr. Sharp did not go gently to his grave.

"Stop dawdling, Mattie," Eliza called from overhead. "Stoke the fire and set a pot of water to boil. Then come up here and fetch these dirty sheets."

We spent the day caring for the Sharp children and reviving Mrs. Sharp, who fainted when the doctor bled both children. After the sun had fallen beneath the rooftops, we arrived at the Collbran house in time to see the body of the last Collbran taken out to the death cart.

Eliza dragged me inside, saying we still had an obligation to wash down the sickroom.

We closed the door behind us when the western sky was shot through with the last pewter and gold rays of the day.

"You go on home, Mattie, you need a good meal and a rest," Eliza said. "I only have one more house on this list. Tell Joseph that I'll be along just as soon as I'm finished."

"No," I said firmly. "I'm not going anywhere. The work will go faster if you have me there, and you shouldn't walk home alone after dark."

Eliza raised an eyebrow.

"Never knew you to look for extra work. Come along then."

We walked in silence, east first, then north. I followed closely, not wanting to lose Eliza in the confusion of alleys and shortcuts.

"I haven't been here before," Eliza said. "Another member of the Society asked that I stop in before retiring. These women are seamstresses, they live alone." She knocked politely on the peeling door, then entered.

The Gundy sisters were both mending. They silently drank their broth and nibbled on the bread. Eliza helped each woman walk to the necessary and back while I aired out their mattresses. We washed the sisters' thin bodies and pulled clean shifts over their heads. One of the women tried to press coins into Eliza's hand, but

Eliza politely refused and put the money back in the sisters' shabby purse.

My stomach grumbled as we mounted the stairs of the cooperage. I wondered what Joseph had cooked. He didn't have Eliza's cooking skills, but I wasn't fussy. Eliza breathed heavily as she labored ahead of me. How many more days could we carry on like this?

The front room was dark except for the flicker of a small fire in the hearth. No suppertime smells welcomed us. I looked around for the twins and Nell. A log popped and the sound echoed around the apartment like a gunshot.

Joseph sat next to the fire, his face in his hands. He did not look up as we entered.

"Joseph?" Eliza called sharply. "Joseph, what ails you? Are you feverish again? Are you chilled?"

Joseph raised his face to look at his sister. Tears coursed down his cheeks. He couldn't bring himself to speak.

Eliza grabbed his shoulders and shook him.

"What happened?" she shouted. "Where is Robert? Where are William and Nell?"

Joseph wiped the back of his hand across his eyes. I stepped back from the sadness in his face; it filled the room and threatened to pull me in. He pointed to the bedchamber.

The twins lay next to each other on the bed, their eyes closed. They panted heavily as if they had just come in from a romp outside. Nell lay on her pallet on the floor. She was feverish, but slept soundly.

"Oh, sweet Jesus, not these little boys!" cried Eliza. "Open that window farther, Mattie. We need some air in here."

"It's already open all the way," I answered.

"It can't be," Eliza snapped. "It's hot enough to roast a duck in here."

She shouldered me aside and pushed up the sash herself. It would go no farther.

"Do you want me to boil water?" I asked.

"Yes. No!" Eliza spun so that her skirts flared, and clenched her fists against her head. "We can't have a fire in here. The boys won't be able to breathe if it gets any hotter. Dear God, why take these children? I promised I wouldn't let them die."

I stood in the doorway, not sure what to do next. Joseph hadn't moved from his stool. Robert moaned and reached his arm out until he found William. Eliza sat down and stroked Robert's forehead. She squeezed her eyes and covered her mouth as she struggled to control her anguish.

"It's cooler up at Bush Hill," I said.

"They don't have room," Eliza said fiercely.

"But it's cooler there," I repeated. "The rooms have many windows that catch the wind. It's clean, and they have French physicians."

Eliza shook her head. "We have to do it ourselves.

We will find a way to make them well again."

I looked across the small room. The sound of the river came through the tiny window, along with a distant echo of voices. Windows, I thought. Windows and empty rooms, away from the river, away from the worst heat.

"The coffeehouse," I cried. "Eliza, we'll take them to the coffeehouse!"

CHAPTER TWENTY-FIVE

October 14th, 1793

All is thick and melancholy gloom.
       —Letter of Dr. Benjamin Rush
              Philadelphia, 1793

Mother Smith sent a mule cart to the cooperage. I scrubbed the cart with boiling vinegar while Eliza gathered the drugs and herbs we would use to treat the children. Joseph prayed over his sons and Nell while we packed bed linens and blankets. When the cart was ready, we dragged the mattress down the narrow staircase and laid it in the cart. I carried Nell.

"Mama," she called weakly.

I bit my lip and asked my heart to be hard. I couldn't help her if I fell apart.

Joseph insisted on carrying each boy downstairs by himself, whispering while he tried to massage the pain from his sons' heads. He gently lay them on the mattress and tucked them in so they wouldn't be jostled.

"Take care of them," he said hoarsely to Eliza.

"Aren't you coming?" I asked.

Joseph shook his head. "They have a better chance away from me or anyone with the fever," he said.

"He'll be fine, and those babies will be fine," said Mother Smith resolutely as she patted Joseph's arm. "The Society will watch out for Joseph, Eliza, don't you worry about him. Go on now, go with God."

Joseph's knees buckled slightly as he kissed the boys good-bye, laid his hand on Nell's head, and hugged Eliza. Mother Smith curled her fingers around his elbow. His tall frame leaned against her withered one as Eliza slapped the mule's rump and the wheels of the cart squeaked.

The city was darker than I had ever seen. The moon had already set, but no light flickered in the whale oil lamps that lined High Street. The lamplighters had all fled the city or died. Candlelight spilled from only a few windows, and the stars were faint and distant, as far away as hope or the dawn.

We struggled to get the mattress out of the cart at the coffeehouse. Our arms strained under the awkward weight, dragging it around to the back gate, through the yard, and finally in the back door. At last, we set the mattress and the children on the dusty pine boards of the front room.

"We should keep them down here," I said. "It's too close upstairs and frightfully hot in the day."

"I agree," Eliza said. "But I don't like having the mattress on the floor. Let's push together those tables and set the mattress on top of them."

"Should we open the windows while it is dark? That's how the thieves got in."

Eliza pulled a knife from the waistband of her skirt. "If they try again, we'll be ready."

Once that would have shocked me, but no longer. I picked up the sword and hung it over the fireplace. We would keep the children safe.

Despite the late hour, sleep would not come. Eliza was deep in prayer by the bedside. I felt like an intruder. I fumbled in the clothespress for a candle and set it into a holder on the kitchen wall. The flickering light beat back the darkness. The kitchen looked as it had the night Grandfather died. At least we hadn't suffered any more intruders. My head thumped. So much, so fast. I could not erase visions of the sick and dying. I paced the room. The children slept, Eliza still by their side with her head bent.

I kicked something hard and hurt my toe. What could be on the floor? I got on my hands and knees and felt along the dark floor until I found a lump wrapped in a napkin. I carried it over to the candlelight.

It was Nathaniel's painting, the flowers he sent to me when Mother was ill. I pressed the picture to my cheek. Stay inside, Nathaniel, I thought. Stop tossing flowers out the window at passing girls and stay inside where you are safe.

I smelled the cloth, but found no trace of Mother. Where was she? Was she alive? I had so much to tell her, so much to talk about. I would have traded anything to hear her swift footsteps across the floor. I laid my head on the kitchen table.

As soon as I fell asleep, Eliza nudged my shoulder. "Wake up," she said.

I sprang to my feet and followed her into the front room. "How are they?" I asked.

Eliza opened Robert's eyelids and then William's. Their eyes were bloodshot and yellow-stained.

"They are full of the pestilence," she said grimly. "Nell seems to be faring better, but there is no question she has it too." She pressed her lips together to hold back the tears.

"It will be fine, Eliza. Think of all the people we've cared for. I survived this, Joseph survived, and so did thousands of others. We can do this. I know exactly what you're going to tell me to do. Stoke the fire and prepare to wash more dirty sheets."

Caring for the children was harder than caring for any other patients we had visited. Just as Robert fell asleep, William would wake crying. As soon as he was made comfortable enough to drift off, Robert would stiffen and jolt awake with a piercing scream. Nell didn't recognize me. She woke from terrible dreams and looked around the room blindly, crying for her mother.

Night melted into day. Day surrendered to night.

The small bodies gave off heat like an iron stove no matter what we used to bring down the fever. I hauled up bucket after bucket of cold well water until the rope blistered my hands and the blisters burst and bled. The floor beneath the mattress was a pool of water. We used up all the linens in the house, which I rinsed in vinegar and hung outside to dry.

Eliza fashioned a fan that kept the bugs off the children and cooled them a bit, but it was so large and heavy that we could only wave it for a few minutes at a time. But as soon as we lay the fan down, they would whimper and cry.

The food Mother Smith had hastily packed soon ran low, along with the cask of vinegar that Eliza had brought with us. I kept one eye on the window, watching for a Society member carrying bread or dried meat for them. Eliza was more concerned about the dwindling supply of medicines, the mercury and calomel. She dosed the boys regularly and gently to purge the putrid bile from their bodies, but it seemed to have little effect. The twins cried in pain, in confusion, in terror. It was impossible to give Nell any medicine. We tried forcing it down her mouth, but it came right back up at us. It was all we could do to keep water in her stomach.

On the fourth day—no, it must have been the fifth—an ominous silence pressed in on the room as the fever penetrated deeper. The boys turned frail, their skin ashen and their cheeks sinking, as their bodies burned up under the infection. They didn't have the strength to suck their thumbs. Eliza moved William closer to Robert so they could draw some comfort from each other. Nell lay on her back, her breath coming in shallow pants.

I set the fan on the floor. I had lost track of when I last ate or slept. Eliza picked it up and waved it over the tiny bodies until her arms shook with the effort. She set the fan on the foot of the mattress.

"I think we should find a doctor," Eliza said. "They should be bled."

"No, Eliza, don't bleed them. It will kill them for sure. It won't work."

"I don't like the thought of cutting them either, but it may be our only hope. Dr. Rush recommends it; he was bled himself when he was ill."

"But the French doctors say bleeding kills people. Think of all the patients you've seen who died after the doctors bled them. They didn't bleed me and I'm alive. Don't do it, Eliza."

Eliza stared into the light of the sputtering candle. "They took twenty ounces of blood from Joseph, and he will live for years."

"If Joseph is alive, it is in spite of the bleeding, not because of it." I grabbed Eliza's hands. "Think of it. Dr. Rush has seen two or three epidemics in his life. The French doctors came from the West Indies, where they treat yellow fever every year. Surely their experience is more valuable."

Eliza pulled a hand away and stroked William's arm.

"I don't know what else to do," she whispered. "I promised their mother I wouldn't let them die."

"Trust me. Please," I pleaded. "They'll survive, I know they will. But if we bleed them, we'll deliver them to the grave. We can't cut them, Eliza."

She looked up at me, struggling with her doubts.

"Trust me," I said firmly.

Eliza nodded. "All right. No bleeding."

Robert woke with a shriek that ended all discussion. A few minutes later William woke, vomiting blood and crying. Nell startled and cried weakly. We worked frantically drawing water, washing the burning bodies, and trying every herb, tea, and poultice to break the fever and banish the infection.

The candle burned down to a puddle of wax, then a second and a third. In the stillest hour of the night, the children finally slept, their thin chests barely rising and falling. Eliza sat next to their bed, laid her head on the mattress, and fell asleep instantly. I picked up the bucket to fetch more water in preparation for the next crisis.

I hooked the handle of the bucket onto the rope and let it down into the well. I tried to watch its progress, but it was soon swallowed up in the darkness.

My eyes closed. It was never going to stop. We would suffer endlessly, with no time to rest, no time to sleep.

The thick air clouded my head. The coffeehouse was

silent. The bucket, I thought. I have to bring up the bucket.

I reached for the crank handle. It slipped from my hand as I turned it, and I stumbled backward. I tried again, wrapping both hands around the handle and knitting my fingers together.

The crank stiffened as if it were attached to a mill stone instead of a wooden bucket. I searched for strength somewhere, someplace inside me that had not been starved or fever-burned or beaten or afraid. The crank turned once. Twice. Each turn of the crank took a year of effort, summer, spring, fall and winter, and my tears splashed into the dust as the bucket climbed out of the earth. I pulled it to the side of the well.

Shadows danced into the garden from the candle-light. I followed the jumping light into the garden, where dry stalks pointed to the skies like scrawny fingers, and rotted, wormy vegetables sank into the cracks of the parched soil. We were trapped in a night without end.

I shook my head to clear it of the visions rolling across my mind. Where was the little girl who planted the bean seeds? Where were Mother and Grandfather and the dead mouse that flew out the window a hundred—a thousand—years ago? And Blanchard's yellow silk balloon that tugged against its ropes, hungry to escape the confines of the prison yard. What became of it all?

My eyes closed. I could see that clear January morning, the moment of release when the balloon floated above the rooftops. Thousands of voices cheered and screamed with delight. Nathaniel grasped my hand and we watched as the gold sphere ferried Monsieur Blanchard and his little black dog away on the wind. I thought all things were possible in heaven and on earth that day.

A whisper of wind passed by from the north. It lifted the hair off my face and rattled the squash vines. I shivered. Only the soles of my feet were warm, heated by dirt that had absorbed the sun all day. So tired. I laid down between the rows and rested my head on the ground.

CHAPTER TWENTY-SIX

October 23rd, 1793

I think there is now that kind of weather
fermenting which we so much want and has
been so often wished for.
> —Letter of John Walsh, clerk
> Philadelphia, 1793

Something rough lapped at my cheek.
I turned away with a groan.

It followed and rubbed again, like a damp piece of burlap. I pushed it away and came up with a handful of orange fur.

"Silas, go away. Let me sleep. I haven't slept for years."

Silas jumped on me and kneaded with his front paws. The weight on my empty stomach hurt too much. I sat up, my head spinning. My eyes opened slowly, the lashes sticking together. I blinked.

An early winter quill had etched an icy pattern over the garden. My skirt looked as if it had been dusted with fine white flour. I shivered. I was cold. Truly cold, not cold with a fever or grippe. I sneezed and bent to look closely at the white veil that lay over the weeds.

Frost.

"I'm dreaming," I told Silas. The cat ignored me and pounced on a sluggish beetle that lumbered under a leaf. "Starving men dream of food. I dream of frost." I rubbed my eyes and pushed myself to my feet. My back creaked as I rolled my shoulders. I breathed deeply. The cold air chilled my nose and crackled in my lungs.

The fetid stench that had hung over the city for weeks was gone, replaced with brittle, pure air.

I looked around the garden. No insects hovered over the dying plants or the well. The entire yard sparkled with diamonds of frost that quickly melted into millions of drops of water with a gentle kiss of the sun.

Frost.

This was no dream.

"Eliza!! Eliza!!"

Eliza stumbled out onto the porch, alarmed and confused.

"Look, Eliza," I cried. "It's frost! The first frost! The end of the fever!"

She bent down to touch the pale crystals, then rubbed her cold fingertips over her lips.

"Lord have mercy," she whispered. "We made it." She turned to me.

"We made it!"

We flung our arms around each other and jumped up and down, laughing for joy.

"Wait," Eliza said suddenly as she pulled away. "The children. We should bring them out here—let them breathe in the clean air."

"Do you think that's wise? Won't they be chilled?"

"All the work we've done to cool them down and you're worried they might catch a chill? It's just what they need."

The bone-grinding fatigue and numbing hunger of the past weeks evaporated as we carried Grandfather's mattress down from the bedchamber and set it in the middle of the yard. Nell, Robert, and William fussed when they were brought outside, but they sat up enough to drink warm water sweetened with the last of the molasses, then fell asleep as their skin cooled gently.

A messenger from Joseph arrived at midday bearing fresh eggs, pumpkins, three kinds of bread, and a joint of beef. Farmers had come back into town following the frost, and their prices dropped as quickly as the temperature. The messenger cautioned us to stay away from the center of town for another week. There were sure to be new fever cases until summer's grip was well and truly broken.

Eliza told me to eat slowly or I would be sick again. For a change, I listened to her. We fed the children small bits of meat and warm cider. Eliza and I shared a loaf of bread at the kitchen table. Never had such a plain meal brought such satisfaction.

When the children fell asleep after the meal, I took a nap even though it was the middle of the afternoon. I woke to the sound of heavy furniture being dragged across the floor.

"Eliza, what in the name of heaven?"

Eliza looked up. She had pushed the chest of drawers half the distance to the kitchen.

"I've been watching the signs. The way the birch leaves flip in the breeze, the shape of the clouds, and the color of the sun now that it's setting. I predict another frost tonight. We need to get all the furniture outside and expose it to the cold. It's the only way to destroy the pestilence. Come and help me with this chest."

I thought it was a ridiculous notion, but I helped her carry the furniture we could handle outside. The children watched us as if it were completely normal to set furniture outside. Their fevers were broken and their stomachs full. They slept for hours, woke for food, then went back to sleep.

Joseph himself arrived the next morning with the news that the market had reopened. The twins and Nell were resting on the mattress under the cherry tree when he strode across the yard and took all three in his arms. Eliza and I let our tears fall without shame.

Joseph opened the small sack he carried. He took out tops for the boys and a small doll for Nell, toys he had made for them by himself. As the children tried to spin the tops on the lumpy mattress, Joseph joined us on the porch.

He took both Eliza's hands and mine and held them in his. "Thank you," he said. "Thank you for giving me back my boys."

"Balderdash," I said. "Nothing could keep those rapscallions down for long."

"Pour yourself some cider and sit with us," said Eliza.

We sat down comfortably and watched the children play. I poured a second mug of cider.

"You'll hear from your mother soon, I wager," Joseph said.

Eliza shot her brother a warning look, but he ignored it.

"If I were you, I'd head down to the market," he continued. "That's where all the best gossips in town have gathered."

I glanced at Eliza. "May I go?"

"You don't need my permission," Eliza said.

She was right. I could choose for myself.

The market seemed like a festival, its stalls overflowing with food and rejoicing. It was noisier than ever before, talk, talk, talk, friends sharing the news, overblown laughter, strong-lunged farmers bellowing their wares. A welcome wave of noise and good cheer.

I drifted from stall to stall, eavesdropping on good

news and bad. Most of the conversations were about lost relatives and friends. Yellow fever had scattered the residents of Philadelphia to the four winds. No one could guess how long it would take until everyone was accounted for.

"Mattie Cook!" Mrs. Epler cried. "Thanks to Gott you survived. But you are so thin, *liebchen*. You look just like your mother, she works so hard. Here, two fat hens for you and your family. And have some eggs."

"Thank you very much, Mrs. Epler," I said pulling out my purse.

"No, no, no money. My gift," the plump egg seller insisted. "How is Mrs. Cook? Did you go out to the country?"

I laid the dead hens in my basket. "Mother is missing," I said. "Grandfather is dead."

Mrs. Epler's hands flew to her cheeks. "You poor child!" She pulled me close and squeezed me hard, her head barely as high as my shoulder. "Little Mattie, little Mattie."

"It's fine, Mrs. Epler, I'll be fine." I unwrapped her arms from me. "I'm sure Mother will be home soon. But please, ask folks if they've seen her."

"Of course, of course," Mrs. Epler said, bobbing her head up and down. "I'll ask everyone in the whole city."

I had to smile at that. The news would be halfway to New York by nightfall if Mrs. Epler had anything to do with it.

All the farmers were cheerful and generous. I paid very low prices for peaches, carrots, and beets. Though my basket was full, I found room for a sack of hard candy and a small loaf of sugar. "For the children," I told myself.

I had to taste the candy, of course, to make sure it was not stale. I was so vigilant that I tasted several pieces. Nell, Robert, and William deserved the best.

My shopping was done and I had questioned everyone about Mother, but still I lingered, caught between wanting to leave and wanting to stay until I could sort out the thoughts battling in my head.

What now? Should I travel to the Ludingtons' farm? Wait in town a few more days?

I looked over a selection of bruised apples. Part of me did not want to know what had happened. If Mother was dead, I'd have to sell the coffeehouse, or have the orphan's court sell it for me. I'd get work as a scullery maid, or move into the orphanage and do laundry.

I looked past the apple seller to the haberdasher's window behind him. My face looked back at me from the thick glass. Mrs. Epler was right: I was thin. Yellow fever had certainly done away with vanity. I lifted my chin. The shape of my face looked for all the world like Mother's, her nose, her mouth.

But my eyes were my own. I blinked.

A scullery maid? Ridiculous. I was Matilda Cook, daughter of Lucille, granddaughter of Captain William

Farnsworth Cook, of the Pennsylvania Fifth Regiment. I could read, write, and figure numbers faster than most. I was not afraid of hard work.

I would set my own course.

Someone placed a hand on my elbow.

"I hoped I might find you here," a low voice rumbled in my ear.

My heart jumped.

"Nathaniel!"

I wanted to throw my arms around him, or jump up and down, or . . . I wasn't sure what I wanted to do. I wanted to stop blushing. I tried to collect myself.

"How are you?" I asked. *Think of something intelligent,* I commanded myself. *Don't be a ninny.*

A slow smile spread across his face. Had he grown even taller?

"Much better now that I've found you," he said. His hand stayed on my elbow. "I'm sorry I didn't bring you flowers."

"That's all right," I said, a ridiculous smile on my face. "I have your painting on the mantle. It was beautiful. You look . . . quite well. Did you have the fever?"

"No. We were most fortunate."

His hand was still on my elbow, warm and friendly. I liked having it there.

"Why don't I walk you home?" he suggested.

We walked slowly. Step, step, stop and talk. Step, step, stop and talk. His voice had a low, sweet note in it like a cello, and his smile lit up every shadow. I stopped worrying about being a ninny.

"I wanted to jump out the window when I saw you a few weeks ago," he said. "I thought you were safely in the country."

"I was staying with Eliza and her family," I explained. "The coffeehouse had been broken into by intruders."

He lifted my chin. "You look like you need a week's worth of cakes. Didn't Eliza feed you?"

"There wasn't much food for anyone," I said. "What about you? What did you eat?"

"You know Mr. Peale. He always does things in a unique way. You've heard of the collection of animals he has?"

I nodded. Mr. Peale had opened a natural history museum in his house.

"We ate the specimens he had collected, before they were treated with arsenic and stuffed, of course."

"No! You didn't!"

"Yes, we did. And I'll never eat possum again, I promise you," said Nathaniel. "Disgusting. It was as much Master Peale's good humor that kept us going as much as anything."

He stopped. We were in front of the coffeehouse.

"Some days felt like we were trapped in a night-mare," he said.

"It's hard to believe it's really over," I said. "It feels so strange, so sudden. We're supposed to go back to the way we lived before, but everything has changed."

"The important things haven't changed at all," Nathaniel said. He stole an apple from my basket and took a bite. "I will always snatch apples from your basket, you have my solemn word."

A carriage turned off High Street and stopped halfway down the block. The door opened and out popped the head of Mrs. Henning, my neighbor, wearing an absurd feathered hat. Her children poured out behind her and rushed the door of their house. It looked like they were returning from nothing more serious than an afternoon's drive in the country.

"Your mother will be home soon," Nathaniel said confidently. "She'll chase me off the front porch and try to marry you to a lawyer."

"I won't let her," I said, standing taller.

Nell squealed in the house and the twins laughed. Nathaniel and I had suddenly run out of things to say.

"Well, I should go home," he mumbled. "I may stop in from time to time. Make sure you're well."

"That would be nice," I said.

"Don't worry. She'll be home soon."

I tried to smile. No matter how kind he was, it couldn't erase the question that had haunted me all afternoon.

What if she didn't come home at all?

CHAPTER TWENTY-SEVEN

October 30th, 1793

Blessed be God for the change in the weather. The disease visibly and universally declines.

—Dr. Benjamin Rush
Letter, 1793

Nathaniel was a constant caller that week. Mr. Peale had given him a free rein to wander and enjoy himself after being cooped up in the house. Nathaniel said all of the Peales were outside as much as possible. He predicted that the painting family would soon produce a number of landscapes.

As word of the frost spread, hundreds of people swarmed into town. The returnees were all well-fed. They called to each other in annoying, bright voices. I wanted to tell them to hush. It felt like they were dancing on a grave with no thought to the suffering they had escaped. Those of us who had remained behind were gaunt and pale. People who were dosed with mercury spat frequently and covered their mouths to hide their blackened teeth.

Eliza reminded me not to be bitter, but it was hard.

With every hour that passed, Philadelphia shed the appearance of a ghost city and looked more and more like the capital of the United States. Like a wilted flower stuck in a bowl of water, it drew strength and blossomed. Nathaniel talked about painting the rebirth of the city. I thought he would do a grand job.

Nathaniel and I walked outside together as often as possible. My favorite time was just before sundown, when the dinner dishes were washed and the children ready for bed. Nathaniel would pass by the front door at just the right time. I would pretend to be surprised to see him, and he would feign shock that a busy girl like me had time for a stroll.

The first few walks only took us a few blocks and back. Then we went as far as the giant burial ground where Grandfather rested. The dirt had been smoothed over and grass had already started growing in patches. I tried to remember exactly where he lay, but it looked different without the confusion of grave diggers and heaps of earth.

"Don't fret," Nathaniel said. "We know he's here. He wouldn't want you to fuss about a headstone anyway."

I nodded. "Maybe it's better that he's buried here. He would want to be in as large a crowd as possible. I bet there are more of his friends here than in the cemetery."

"And he'll hear better stories," he said.

We turned to walk home.

"Any news?" he asked.

I shook my head. "I've written several letters, but they're useless until the post office opens. The newspaper won't run any advertisements before the end of the year."

"Don't give up hope."

It was Eliza's idea to have a small feast of thanksgiving with Joseph and the boys. I suggested Mother Smith, too. We didn't need to discuss Nathaniel. Of course he would come.

Keeping the children out of the kitchen while we were cooking reminded me of trying to catch fish in my petticoat. No matter how I tried to get hold of the giggling twins, they always slipped away. Nell was the sneaky one. She waited until my hands were full with the boys, then stole a bite from the table. I finally filled the butter churn and set it on the back porch. I told them they would get a wonderful treat just as soon as they turned that milk into butter. That kept them busy for a while.

At long last we sat down to a table filled with food.

Mother Smith blessed the meal. "Dear Lord, we give thanks for your blessings. For bringing us through these days of pestilence, we thank you. For saving our children, we thank you. For restoring us, for watching over us, for giving us this bounty, we thank you. Watch over those who have passed, Lord."

"Watch my Betty," Joseph said, his voice cracking. The twins looked on as their father fought to control his grief. Though we were all healed of the fever, some wounds were inside the heart and would mend slowly.

"Keep them close until we are ready to join them," Mother Smith concluded. "Blessed be Thy name. Amen."

We were solemn and quiet for a moment, but three hungry children soon distracted us. It was time to feast.

"I had forgotten what it felt like to sit down to a proper meal," said Joseph as he cut the beef on William's plate. "This is a mighty spread."

"You set a good table, for a girl," said Mother Smith.

"Hardly a girl anymore," remarked Eliza.

"I couldn't have done it without your help," I said. "I've been very lucky."

"You made your luck," corrected Mother Smith.

"Ummmh," mumbled Nathaniel. I thought he was agreeing, but his mouth was so full it was hard to tell. He reached for more potatoes and winked at me.

"Any news from your mother?" asked Joseph. "Seems to me that . . ."

Eliza shoved a bowl of beans at Joseph to cut him off. I knew what he was about to say. He thought Mother had died. So did Eliza.

"She'll be back soon," said Mother Smith as she spooned more carrots onto her plate. "I can feel it in my bones and they never lie. Stop fretting and pass me the butter."

A contented silence settled over the table as everyone ate their fill. It wasn't until I set out the pies for dessert that Joseph spoke again.

"Have you decided your price, Matilda?"

"What price?"

"The price for the coffeehouse. You've got a good spot here. You sell this place, you'll get enough money to set you up nice."

"Joseph!" Eliza scolded her brother.

"What?" he protested. "She has to be practical. What's she going to do?"

"She could work with Mrs. Peale," suggested Nathaniel.

"The Lord will work it out," Mother Smith said.

"The Lord helps those who help themselves," Joseph said. "It's no use pretending. This business needs to be sold for Mattie's dowry, and Eliza here has to find a new job."

"Eliza could work for Mrs. Peale, too," said Nathaniel. "They are in desperate need of a good cook. The other one quit after the possum."

"Mind your own business, boy," Eliza snapped.

"He's just trying to help," Joseph said. "We're all trying to help."

Everyone thought they knew what was right for me. It was just like listening to Mother and Grandfather making the decisions while I stood to the side. I put down my knife. This would not do. It was time to bring out the plan that had hatched days earlier when I saw my face in the window.

"I'm not selling," I said loudly.

The argument stopped and everyone looked at me.

"I'm going to open the coffeehouse for business. Tomorrow."

"More the fool you, then," replied Joseph. "You'll never run it on your own."

"I don't have to," I answered. "I'm taking on a partner."

"A partner? Who?" asked Eliza. She glared at Nathaniel, who shook his head.

"Not me," he said quickly.

"What do you know about taking on a partner?" Eliza asked.

"Plenty," I said. "My partner has to be someone I can trust. Someone who knows how to run a coffeehouse and isn't afraid to give me a kick in the backside every now and then to keep me on the right path."

Eliza set her fork down. "Speak plainly, child. I'm not fond of riddles."

I swallowed.

"Eliza, I want you be my partner. There's no one better suited to it, no one I can trust. Or who will put up with me."

Even Nell sat quietly.

"Mattie, I don't have the money to buy a partnership from you. It's kind of you to ask, but I can't."

"No, oh no, you don't understand. I couldn't take your money. I'm sharing it with you. It's the right thing to do, and it's good business."

Eliza started to speak, but the words wouldn't come.

This was not what I had expected. She was supposed to say yes, and then we would dance a jig.

"It won't work," Eliza said.

"We'll make it work," I countered.

"It wouldn't be right," Eliza answered.

"Don't . . . don't you want to work here?" I asked. "I know Joseph needs you to help with the boys. They could stay here with us. And Nell. This way Nell can stay with us, too. It's the perfect solution."

Crack!

Mother Smith banged her cane so hard on the floor that it dented the board.

"She'll take it," said Mother Smith firmly. "And no nonsense from you," she added as she wagged her finger at Eliza. "It's an opportunity, one you deserve, one offered from the heart. I know you, Eliza, you'll worry about shillings and pence. So save from your share of the earnings and pay out of that. She'll take it."

"You'll need a lawyer to write it out," said Joseph gravely.

"No, we don't," I said. "I couldn't cheat Eliza, I can barely sneak a piece of cheese from the larder without feeling bad."

Joseph smiled. "I wasn't thinking of you. I was

thinking about others. Some folk will say Eliza took advantage of you. They don't like to see black people move up."

"Joseph's right," said Mother Smith. "People love to talk. So you'll do it by the law, with lawyers and wax seals and all. Say yes, Eliza, so I can eat my pie."

Eliza looked around the table.

"It doesn't seem I have a choice," Eliza said. I leaned over and wrapped my arms around her. Nathaniel lifted his cider mug to toast the two of us.

A rapid knock at the front door broke up the celebration.

"I'll get it," I said. "Eat up, everyone. There's more in the kitchen."

A messenger stood at the door, hat in hand. "Excuse me, Ma'am," he said. "I'm to ask for the proprietor of Cook's."

I cleared my throat and smoothed my skirt.

"I am one of the owners. What can I do for you?"

The boy held out a bulging sack.

"My master, Jasper Blake, asked that I bring you these coffee beans and mention that his warehouse is open for business."

He handed me the sack.

"We expect a ship soon out of Liverpool carrying the finest teas and beans. Your business will be appreciated."

"I know the name of your master well," I replied. "You may convey my thanks to him. I am pleased that he has come through the plague days. Tell him I look forward to examining his goods."

The boy grinned as I slipped him a coin.

As I returned to the table, Nathaniel stood up and imitated me, pretending to smooth a skirt and fix his hair. "You may convey my thanks," he teased.

"Stop," I laughed. "If I'm going to help run this place I had better act the part." I covered my mouth and giggled. It did feel a bit like play-acting.

"Better get used to that," said Joseph. "When word gets out that the Cook Coffeehouse is open for business again, you won't be able to keep tradesmen or customers away!"

CHAPTER TWENTY-EIGHT

November 10th, 1793

Many stores are lately opened and the city exhibits a scene of increasing trade and bustle.
——Letter of John Walsh, clerk
Philadelphia, 1793

Three days after we opened for business, every chair in the front room was filled, the air thick again with arguments, tobacco smoke, and the smell of fresh coffee and cakes. Eliza was in the kitchen cooking up a storm, and the room had never been cleaner. Mother would have been very proud.

I carried a tray above my head. "Who wants to try some apple cake? A free sample!" I offered.

"Over here, Mattie, over here!" The shouts came from all directions.

I smiled. Free samples were proving a clever way to get the customers to eat more. Feed them one bite and they'd pay for three more. I quickly distributed the small pieces of apple cake and went through refilling coffee mugs.

"Another cup?" I asked. I picked up a mug in front of a doctor studying the chess board.

He nodded, deep in concentration. He kept his finger on his queen, in danger of being captured by his opponent's pawn. "Could I get some soup, too?" he asked. "This match is far from over."

"Me, too," said his companion.

"How about some mutton stew?" I asked.

"Perfect. Ha!" The doctor rescued the queen by moving his knight.

"Scoundrel," muttered the other man.

"Right away, Sir," I said, picking up the tray.

Eliza and Nathaniel sat in the kitchen. He had stepped in to help us with errands since we opened. He was also Eliza's taste-tester.

"We need more stew," I said. "Two bowls."

She shook her head. "This keeps up and we'll be serving breakfast, too!"

"I have plenty of ideas," I assured her. "What if we baked small cakes and delivered them to the State House with a handbill advertising our new wares?"

Eliza frowned.

"How many cakes? The price of sugar is still high. How about apple bread instead? That's cheaper to make."

Nathaniel cleared his throat. "I could paint a sign that you could put out front. I could make a design for the handbill, too."

"And I suppose we'll pay you in cakes, right?" I joked.

"That would suit me fine." He rose from his chair. "I have to go to Peale's. See you tomorrow."

Eliza waited until he had gone. "He's useful, for a painter."

I smiled. "Where are the children?"

"Sleeping, thank goodness," Eliza said. "When they wake up, I'm going to set them to work churning butter again. That kept you and Polly out of trouble when you were small."

I nodded. "I want to visit Polly's mother on Sunday. Don't let me forget. Now I need two bowls of mutton stew."

When I had served the stew and filled up the next round of empty cups, I surveyed the room. It was brighter with Nathaniel's paintings on the walls. He had already sold two. Watson next door was interested in selling his lot, but I couldn't afford to build an addition to the coffeehouse, not yet. Maybe by spring. The weather would be better then, anyway.

Everything was going the way I had planned, but I felt hollow. The outside of my life was sound. Eliza and I had the coffeehouse. Nathaniel and I had an understanding. Nell would stay. I was still a long way away from being able to travel to Paris, but it would happen someday.

And yet . . .

The fever lingered. Grandfather's chair by the hearth stood empty. The parrot's cage was gone. The ghosts of friends lost in the last months flitted across when I least expected them. And then there was the ache I avoided most of all.

The front door swung open with a crash. All conversation ceased.

It was Nathaniel, struggling to catch his breath.

"It's the president!" he said. "President Washington. He's returned. He's coming down High Street right now!"

The men all abandoned their chairs at once and fought to get out the door. I looked back in the kitchen.

"I've got a cake rising," Eliza said. "I'm not leaving that for any man. You go on."

"Come on, Mattie!" Nathaniel called. "Hurry!"

High Street was already lined with people, all peering anxiously up the road. Nathaniel grabbed my hand and pulled me along until we found a break in the crowd.

"There he is!" someone shouted.

"Huzzah! Huzzah! General George is back!" The crowd roared in approval. Men took off their hats and waved them, women fluttered handkerchiefs, and children jumped up and down.

A group of three riders proceeded down the middle of the street.

"Advisors," Nathaniel said. "They don't count. Look, there he is."

The president rode a few paces behind, calmly smiling and waving at the crowd. He rode his beautiful white horse, reins in one hand, his hat in the other. He nodded to the crowd with a dignified air. If Grandfather were here, he'd be busting his buttons by now.

I never thought Washington was handsome, but on that horse, he looked like something special. He was our leader. The crowd continued cheering and waving until he was far down the block. If the president was back, then the fever was truly over. If the president was back, we were safe.

I threw my arms around Nathaniel and planted a big kiss on his cheek.

He pulled back in surprise.

"Do you always do that when the president rides by? If so, I'll take a job working for him."

I blushed and looked down at my feet.

"I'm just happy," I said.

The crowd was thinning. Some people followed down High Street, others went back to what they had been doing. My afternoon customers hurried back to the coffeehouse. That was a comforting sight.

Nathaniel pointed back up the road. "Who do you think all of those people are?"

Following behind the president's entourage came a scraggly parade of wagons and carriages.

"Members of the cabinet?" I ventured.

A man standing next to us shook his head. "No. Them's the folks that waited. They waited until General George came back. Knew it would be safe then, the fever gone."

One of the carriages turned off High Street and stopped in front of the coffeehouse.

"Time to get back to work, Miss Cook," Nathaniel said. "Look, you've got another customer."

The driver and a woman dressed in country clothes were gently helping a frail woman with gray in her hair step out of the carriage. She leaned heavily on their arms. When her feet were on the ground, she raised her face to us. Tired, familiar, beautiful.

Mother had come home.

CHAPTER TWENTY-NINE

November 10th, 1793

The yellow fever will discourage the growth
of great cities in our nation.
—Thomas Jefferson
Letter to Dr. Benjamin Rush, 1800

I dashed across the street without looking.

"Mother!"

I gathered her into my arms. She felt like a frail bird. We stood in silence, rocking and holding onto each other as if the rest of the world didn't matter. Which was true.

At last she pulled away from me with a sigh.

"I need to sit down," she said with a weak smile. "Where are my manners? Matilda, this is my good friend Mrs. Ludington."

I curtsied out of habit. "You've been with the Ludingtons the whole time?"

Nathaniel stepped forward. "Good day, Mrs. Cook. It is a pleasure to see you survived the terrible pestilence.

Why don't go we inside where you'll be more comfort-able?"

"What a good idea," Mother said. "Nathaniel Benson, that's your name?"

"Yes, Ma'am," he said. Very respectful, very smart.

I waited for her to make a sharp-tongued remark, but she didn't.

Mother could not walk unaided. Mrs. Ludington took one arm and I took the other to help her. Nathaniel walked ahead and opened the door for us.

As we crossed the threshold, the company in the front room fell silent. They were all as shocked by Mother's appearance as I was. The doctor at the chess-board stood in respect. His companion did the same, then every man in the room rose to his feet to honor her.

She paused for a moment. "Thank you, gentlemen."

"Lucille!" Eliza stood in the kitchen doorway, her hand covering her mouth. She took two steps and hugged Mother, tears flowing freely and without apology.

"Oh, my Lord," she said, wiping away the tears. "Let's get into the kitchen."

I helped Mother sit at the kitchen table. Mrs. Ludington sat across from her. Eliza quickly poured coffee for all of us, then grabbed a serving tray.

"You stay here and catch up," she commanded me. "I'll take care of the front room. If I get desperate, I'll use that painter of yours."

Mother picked up her mug, her hand shaking. She sipped once, then set the mug down. It seemed too heavy for her to hold.

There were so many questions, so much to say. Where should I start?

"Do you feel well?" I asked.

She nodded once. "I require a nap these days," she said with a hint of her old self. "Imagine that, if you will."

"Your mother is still recovering," Mrs. Ludington explained. "The doctors say it's a miracle she survived at all."

"Bunkum," Mother said.

Mrs. Ludington smiled. "It's not bunkum, Lucille." She turned to me. "Your mother joined us at the farm a few days after she sent you and your grandfather on. When she realized you were lost, she went wild."

"I was concerned," Mother said.

"We tried to keep her in bed, it was clear she was still quite ill. We sent messages to every town we could think of, but those who bothered to reply had not seen you. Lucille was frantic. She rose at midnight and took one of our horses to search for you herself. We found her two days later, near death at the side of the road. It took weeks for her to recover."

"I'm much better now," Mother said.

Mrs. Ludington shook her head in disagreement. "We came when we heard that President Washington was returning. Lucille said that would be the sign that your Grandfather was waiting for. Where is the Captain? I didn't see him when we came in."

"He died," I said flatly.

"Oh. Oh, my. I'm so sorry," Mrs. Ludington said.

Mother looked into the fire. I waited for her questions, but there were none.

"Did the doctor prescribe any treatments for you, Mother?" I asked.

Mrs. Ludington jumped in. "She is supposed to live a life of leisure, those were his exact words. The second attack nearly took her off to join your father. It damaged her heart." She arched her eyebrows. "She won't be able to run the coffeehouse anymore. She should sell it and buy a small house near us."

Mother pressed her lips together tightly.

"We'll talk about that later," I said quickly. "Can I get you something to eat, Mrs. Ludington? Some stew?"

The farmer's wife stood up. "I promised my husband I would return today, and it is a long ride back. I must go."

I tried to convince her to stay the night, or at least take a meal with us, but she was determined. She bent over and hugged Mother briefly, said good-bye to me, and left.

I peeked in the front room. A few customers had left; the rest were smoking their pipes and enjoying their conversation.

Mother coughed. "Is this your work or Eliza's?" she asked.

"Mine," I said as I sat down across from her. "I wanted to open again. Eliza wanted me to sell."

The clock ticked.

"William is dead, then?"

The clock ticked again, then rang the hour. I waited until the noise stopped.

"Yes. In September."

"Oh, Mattie." Tears welled in Mother's eyes. "Dear God, I was so worried. I couldn't find you, no matter where I looked. I searched and searched until I fell ill again. I couldn't sleep, I was so afraid you were . . ."

"I'm fine, I'm fine. Shh. Please don't cry. Everything is better now. I'm home, you're home. You don't have to worry anymore." I drew up a chair next to her, and she leaned against my shoulder. I cradled her head in my arms until her sobs quieted.

"Tell me how you fared," she said. "I can remember so little, and I've lost track of all the weeks."

I told her everything, from the time the death cart dumped her at the front door to the first frost. I didn't give her all the details of the intruders or the night Grandfather died. There would be time for that later when she felt stronger.

Mother's eyes drifted back to the fire burning in the hearth. Her hands lay in her lap, withered and limp. I had never seen her hands stay still before. They had always been busy with cleaning or needlework or polishing.

I had a sudden sense of what was to come and I blinked away the tears.

"Help me upstairs, Mattie," Mother said. "I need to rest."

December 11th, 1793

*. . . [We] are devoutly to acknowledge that
kind Providence . . . hath restored our city to
its useful state of health and prosperity.*
 —Petition of Citizens to the
 Council of Philadelphia, 1793

I opened one eye. A scratching noise in the corner of
the room had woken me, the scrambling feet of a
desperate mouse about to become breakfast for a lumpy
orange cat. I winced as Silas pounced. The squeaking
stopped.

I rolled over to look out the window. It was dark still.
The faint call of a watchman could be heard down
Seventh Street, and a few stars hung still in the sky. I
burrowed beneath the warm weight of my quilt. My toes
curled at the thought of crossing the icy floorboards on
a dark December morning.

Nothing gained by delay, I thought. No one else is
going to get the house stirring. I snatched my stockings

off the stool next to my bed and pulled them on under the covers, taking care not to disturb Nell, who slept beside me. Thank goodness she had learned not to wet the bed before the weather turned cold. I tucked the quilt around her and stood up, quickly changing into my clean day shift. I stepped into my woolen overskirts, laced my stays, and wrapped a heavy shawl over my bodice.

Mother rolled over and snored quietly. She had coughed late into the night. It was good for her to sleep peacefully. I nudged Silas with my toe. The cat daintily picked up his breakfast and made for the stairs.

I crossed the hall to the other bedchamber. Eliza stirred in her sleep, mumbling about ginger and nutmeg. Robert and William slept soundly, their arms wrapped around each other in their trundle bed, their chests rising and falling in unison. I crept down the stairs, careful to skip the squeaky ones.

I dug out the embers from the ashes of the kitchen fireplace and laid tinder on them. The dry wood caught quickly and the flames soon warmed my face and hands. I swung the kettle over the flames and looked into the fire while the water heated.

Eliza would want to send the twins to fetch the day's newspapers. Mother would fuss, of course. She didn't think they were old enough to do anything besides raise a ruckus in the garden. The sooner we could afford a pony and cart, the better. That way Mother could run errands together with the boys, and Eliza and I could get some work done in peace. It would be nice to finish putting by the mincemeat before the snow came for good. Nell still refused to leave my side, but I didn't mind.

The water finally boiled. I made a coffee for myself, a mug for Eliza, and one for Mother. I cut a lump of sugar off the loaf and added it along with a healthy dollop of milk to my mug. Being the first one awake did bring some privileges, I thought with a smile.

Overhead, footsteps crossed the room. I hurried to set out the breakfast dishes before Eliza came downstairs. She didn't begrudge me a few minutes of quiet, but the table-setting came first.

When the crockery was laid out, I carried my mug through the front room, past the polished tables and backgammon boards, past the beautiful new painting of a meadow full of flowers. I backed up to adjust the painting so it hung nice and straight. Nathaniel was coming along nicely, Mr. Peale said. Three years, maybe four, and he would be able to support himself. That wasn't long to wait.

I opened the front door and sat on the step facing High Street. A lamplighter some blocks down reached up with his long pole to extinguish the street lamp. To the east, beyond the river, the stars faded before the promise of a new day.

These solitary minutes each morning were fast

becoming a habit. A good habit, but one I would soon need a woolen cloak to enjoy. The sky brightened to a dull bronze glow as the last of the season's geese rushed southward, flying so low I could hear the beat of their wings against the morning air. I drained the mug reluctantly and scraped my finger along the bottom to get the last of the undissolved sugar.

Looking down the peaceful street, it seemed no one could imagine the terror we had all endured. There were many tables with empty places or invalids who had once been as strong as horses, but the sun continued to rise. People filled the street each day. On Sunday the church bells rang. Philadelphia had moved on.

Early morning was the only time I felt as if there were ghosts nearby, memories of the weeks of fear. That's when I found myself listening for Polly's giggle or Grandfather's voice. Sometimes they felt so close. Close enough to tell me I should stop dawdling and get to work.

I smiled as the mist faded. The yellow sun rose, a giant balloon filled with prayers and hopes and promise. I stood and shook the idleness out of my skirts.

Day was begun.

APPENDIX

DID THE EPIDEMIC REALLY HAPPEN?

Absolutely. The yellow fever outbreak that struck Philadelphia in 1793 was one of the worst epidemics in United States history. In three months it killed nearly five thousand people, 10 percent of the city's population.

Thousands of people fled to escape the disease. Congress adjourned on schedule and its members left town, along with George Washington and Thomas Jefferson. Mayor Matthew Clarkson was one of the few high-ranking government officials courageous enough to stay. He and the members of the Mayor's Committee tried to hold the city together as the death toll mounted.

BATTLE OF THE DOCTORS

Medicine in the late 1700s was crude. The stethoscope had not yet been invented, nor had the thermometer. People did not understand how disease was spread.

At the beginning of the epidemic there were about eighty people practicing medicine in Philadelphia. Not all of them were trained doctors. Some fled to the countryside, others died of yellow fever.

The doctors of Philadelphia battled one another as well as the epidemic. They were loosely divided into two camps: the followers of Dr. Benjamin Rush, and the followers of French physicians like Dr. Jean Deveze.

Dr. Rush was one of the most famous doctors in the country. He gave patients mercury, calomel, and jalap to make them throw up and have diarrhea. He drained blood from them (a common practice) to get rid of the "pestilence" in their bodies. Medical experts speculate that Rush's treatments killed many of his patients.

The French doctors prescribed rest, fresh air, and lots of fluids. That was the best way to treat the disease. It still is.

TAKE TWO SPONGES AND
CALL ME IN THE MORNING

Philadelphians were desperate for anything to prevent or cure yellow fever. They soaked sponges in vinegar, then stuck them up their noses. They washed their hair and clothes in vinegar. They even drank it.

Guns and cannons were fired in the street in the hopes that the gunpowder would clean the air. People wore nasty-smelling bags of camphor around their necks, chewed garlic, and drank vile potions of herbs. Beds were buried underground, then dug up in an effort to kill whatever was causing the disease.

Nothing worked. People kept getting sick until the frost killed off the mosquitoes that spread yellow fever.

WHERE ARE THEY BURIED?

Some fever victims were buried in churchyards and cemeteries throughout the city, but many lie anonymously in what is known today as Washington Square, the old potter's field. It is bounded by Sixth, Seventh, Walnut, and Locust Streets in Philadelphia. At one end is the Tomb of the Unknown Soldier, commemorating the Revolutionary War dead buried there. Across Walnut is the former location of the old Walnut Street Jail, where Jean Pierre Blanchard's balloon ascended in January 1793.

THE BALLOON

The first hot-air balloon flown in the United States was launched from the Walnut Street Jail on January 9, 1793, by the French aeronaut Jean Pierre Blanchard. Nearly every person in Philadelphia stopped what they were doing and watched as the yellow silk balloon carried him 5,800 feet in the air.

Blanchard performed several scientific experiments aloft, filling six bottles of air, taking his pulse, and making observations about the air pressure, temperature, and weather. If Benjamin Franklin had lived long enough (he died in 1790), he would have been thrilled with the event.

The wind blew Blanchard fifteen miles, across the Delaware River to New Jersey. Blanchard shared a bottle of wine with the farmer in whose field he landed, and showed the man his "passport," a letter of safe passage written by President George Washington.

A crowd soon gathered, and a wagon was found to transport Blanchard and his deflated balloon back across the river. He was greeted in Philadelphia by a cheering crowd. Blanchard's plans for a second flight in the city were ruined by the yellow fever epidemic.

THE AMAZING PEALE FAMILY

There really was a Peale family, though they did not have an apprentice named Nathaniel Benson. The Peales are sometimes referred to as "the First Family of American Art."

Charles Willson Peale was one of the finest portrait painters in the United States. He was also an intensely curious man. Peale opened America's first natural history museum in his house in the 1780s. His collection included mastodon bones, fossils, minerals, and preserved animals such as jackals, mongooses, and bison, along with dozen of species of amphibians, birds, fish, and insects. After their famous expedition of the newly purchased West (1804–1806), explorers Meriwether Lewis and William Clark donated many of the specimens they had found on their journey to Peale's collection.

Peale fathered seventeen children and named many of them after famous artists. Those who survived childhood became active in the arts or helped their father with the museum. Peale's second son, Rembrandt Peale, was a noted artist who painted his first portrait of George Washington when he was only seventeen. One of his later portraits of Washington hangs in the Smithsonian in the Hall of Presidents. He also painted a well-known portrait of Thomas Jefferson.

FREE AFRICAN SOCIETY

The Free African Society was founded in 1787 by Richard Allen and Absalom Jones. Richard Allen was born a slave in Philadelphia in 1760. He bought his freedom and went on to help found the African Methodist Episcopal Church and become its first bishop. Absalom Jones, born a slave in 1746 and freed in 1784, was the first African-American to be ordained an Episcopal priest. The most widely recognized image of Jones was painted by Raphaelle Peale, the oldest son of Charles Willson Peale.

Allen and Jones founded the society as a mutual aid organization devoted to helping widowed, ill, or out-of-work African-Americans. It was also dedicated to abolishing the evil institution of slavery. Under the leadership of Jones and Allen society members worked day and night to relieve the suffering of yellow fever victims. They nursed the sick, fed them, washed them, buried them, and made sure their orphaned children were cared for.

After the epidemic, society members were attacked in a pamphlet written by publisher Mathew Carey. He accused them of overcharging for burials and stealing from the sick. The charges were lies, and Mayor Matthew Clarkson took out ads in the city's newspapers to defend the heroic work of society members. Allen and Jones wrote their own pamphlet, *A Narrative of the Proceedings of the Black People During the Late Awful Calamity in Philadelphia in 1793*, which described what the African-Americans of Philadelphia had done to help their fellow citizens during the epidemic.

COFFEEHOUSES

Coffeehouses were all the rage in the 1790s. People gathered in them to conduct business, talk politics, and catch up on the news of the day. Owning and running a coffeehouse was considered a respectable business for a widow.

The most famous coffeehouse in Philadelphia was called the London Coffee House (named after—you guessed it—a coffeehouse in London, England). It was opened in 1754 by a printer named William Bradford.

Bradford hung a painting of King George on the wall of his coffeehouse. But when Great Britain started to tax the colonies heavily, the king's picture came down. John Adams, Dr. Benjamin Rush, and other important men met at the London Coffee House to discuss revolutionary strategies. The Declaration of Independence was signed a few blocks away.

THE FRENCH INFLUENCE

France sided with the United States during the American Revolution, sending money and soldiers to aid the young nation. By 1793 the French were having troubles of their own. They beheaded their monarchs—King Louis XVI and his wife, Marie Antoinette—and declared war on England, Spain, and Holland.

Although America was officially neutral, many Americans supported the French. As refugees from the French Revolution and from the slave revolts in the French West Indies poured into Philadelphia, French fashion and language became very popular. Young boys would cheerfully shout, *"Vive la République!"* when they met French sailors in the street. The refugees opened dancing academies, fencing salons, and hairdressing parlors. French cooks introduced ice cream to Philadelphia. Thomas Jefferson's favorite flavor was said to be vanilla. And during the epidemic it was French doctors who had the most effective treatments.

FAMOUS PEOPLE TOUCHED BY THE FEVER

Dolley Payne Todd Madison

Dolley's first husband, John, died during the epidemic of 1793, along with the couple's young son and John's parents. Dolley was later introduced to Congressman James Madison by their mutual friend, Aaron Burr. She married Madison in 1794.

When James Madison was elected the fourth president of the United States in 1809, Dolley became one of the nation's most beloved First Ladies. Among other things, she is famous for organizing the first Easter Egg Roll on the Capitol grounds, and for saving the famous life-size portrait of George Washington when British soldiers burned the White House in 1814.

George Washington

President Washington was in his second term of office when the epidemic hit Philadelphia, then the nation's capital. He left the city on September 10. Why? He said, "Mrs. Washington was unwilling to leave me surrounded by the malignant fever which prevailed, I could not think of hazarding her and the Children any longer by my continuance in the city, the house in which we lived being, in a manner, blockaded, by the disorder."

It was a smart thing to do. Polly Lear, a good friend of Martha Washington's, had contracted yellow fever in the early days of the epidemic. It was said she caught it while shopping in the marketplace with Martha. When Polly died, Thomas Jefferson helped carry her casket at her funeral.

Dr. Benjamin Rush had a young assistant from Virginia named Warner Washington, thought to be a cousin to George Washington. Despite (or because of) Rush's treatment, Warner died of the fever too.

George Washington died on December 14, 1799, of a throat infection.

Dr. Benjamin Rush

Although we know today his methods were useless and dangerous, Dr. Rush's services were in much demand during the fever outbreak. At the height of the epidemic he was seeing 120 patients a day. Dr. Rush contracted the disease himself but survived.

Rush's insistence on perilous remedies for yellow fever patients was a rare misstep for the energetic doctor. He was far ahead of his time on many issues. He fought against slavery and capital punishment, and argued for public schools, the education of girls, and the compassionate treatment of the mentally ill. He treated his insane patients with gentle understanding. Among his mentally ill patients were Mary Girard, wife of Stephen Girard, and a daughter of artist Charles Willson Peale.

Stephen Girard

Born in France, Girard fought on the side of the Americans during the Revolutionary War. He made several fortunes in shipping and banking and was one of the richest men in the country.

Though he could have fled with the other wealthy and influential people during the epidemic, he chose to stay and help. Girard supervised the transformation of Bush Hill into a safe, functioning fever hospital. He came down with the fever himself but survived. Although he trusted his insane wife to Dr. Rush's psychiatric care, he no doubt turned to the French doctors of Bush Hill while he was sick.

TO MARKET, TO MARKET

There were no refrigerators in 1793, no freezers, no twenty-four-hour grocery stores, and no canned hams. Most city dwellers bought their food at the marketplace. Farmers from the countryside would pack their wagons with produce, meat, eggs, cheese, milk, and bread, and drive before sunup into Philadelphia. The people in the city counted on them.

With the government shut down and farmers afraid to come into the city, getting enough food to eat during the epidemic was a problem. It was made worse by the lack of money in the city. In the early days of the epidemic many wealthy people and business owners fled. The people they employed were out of work. It didn't take long until they were out of cash.

All over the East Coast other communities imposed quarantines on people from Philadelphia. That meant that Philadelphians were not allowed to come into their towns, not even to buy food.

We do not have any records that tell us whether or not people starved during the epidemic. We do know that people, especially the poor, were hungry. Some neighboring towns donated food, firewood, and cash to help out. The Mayor's Committee was in charge of collecting and distributing the donations, and the records show that the citizens of Philadelphia were very grateful for them.

THE MIRACULOUS MOVING CAPITAL

Washington, D.C., was not the first capital of the United States. In fact, the capital moved all over the place before settling down on the banks of the Potomac River in 1800.

The Continental Congress met for the first time in Philadelphia in 1774. It was the largest city in the colonies and centrally located. Philadelphia remained the base of the government for years, but the Revolutionary leaders were occasionally chased out by British soldiers. The Congress moved to Baltimore and Annapolis, Maryland; Lancaster and York, Pennsylvania; and Princeton and Trenton, New Jersey. While on the run the Congress met in courthouses, taverns, and private homes.

After the peace treaty was signed with the British, the new American government set up shop in New York City. George Washington's first inauguration took place there on April 30, 1789.

While the government was based in New York, there were fierce debates about where the permanent home of the nation's capital should be. Southerners wanted the capital to be located farther south. Alternatives were named: Wilmington, Delaware; Lancaster, Pennsylvania; Annapolis or Baltimore, Maryland. None passed.

Finally discussion centered around building the capitol on the Potomac River. It was a geographic compromise between North and South, and it was easily reachable by boat, an important consideration in the days when roads were often impassable. After much debate the Congress decided to carve a piece out of Maryland and Virginia and create a federal district. They did not want the seat of national government to be located in any one state, afraid that the other states would think it unfair. Philadelphia was the temporary home of the government from 1790 to 1800. In 1800 the government moved to the District of Columbia.

After leaving Philadelphia in the middle of the yellow fever epidemic, George Washington headed south. He laid the cornerstone for the United States Capitol on September 18, 1793.

FEAR AND PANIC

At the beginning of the epidemic most people in Philadelphia were calm. There had been "fevers" in the city before, and few thought it was anything to worry about. But as the death toll quickly rose panic took over.

The fever closed businesses and the government. All anyone could talk about was "Who's dead? Who's sick?" The men pushing handcarts carrying corpses to the burial grounds called out, "Bring out your dead!" just as they had during the bubonic plague in England.

Although it can be hard for us to imagine, there are many reports of sick people being abandoned by their families, some thrown into the street to die. Friends and neighbors stopped talking and avoided one another on the street. Kindness seemed to evaporate. In a few short weeks the city was transformed into a living nightmare, with the sick dying, the healthy paralyzed with fear, and the doctors helpless.

The brave people who stayed in the city and helped the sick were extraordinary. The volunteers of the Free African Society, those who worked at Bush Hill, and the members of the Mayor's Committee devoted themselves with incredible courage to care for strangers. They are the real heroes of this story.

YELLOW FEVER TODAY

Yellow fever still exists, but not in the United States. In 1902 Dr. Walter Reed discovered that the female *Aedes aegypti* mosquito spreads the disease. In the 1930s a vaccine was developed, but yellow fever still kills thousands of people a year in sub-Saharan Africa and parts of South America.

Acknowledgements

My deepest thanks to The Historical Society of Pennsylvania, one of the oldest historical societies in the United States. Most of the research for this book was done in their excellent collection of newspapers, diaries, letters, and account books written during the yellow fever epidemic of 1793.

Although writing is done in solitude, it was my good fortune to work with and be supported by a wonderful group of people as I researched and wrote this book. My humble appreciation and gratitude to all:

Anna "Coxie" Cox Toogood, Historian of Independence National Park, Philadelphia, and Gretchen Worden, Director, Mutter Museum of the College of Physicians of Philadelphia. Both of these authorities on the 1793 epidemic meticulously checked the manuscript for historical errors and pesky anachronisms. Any factual errors or historical misinterpretations that crept into the book despite their vigilance are the responsibility of the author.

Janet Theophano, Ph.D., Assistant Director, College of General Studies of the University of Pennsylvania and professor of folklore, who wisely counseled me about the roles of women in the 1790s and directed me to the hidden treasures of recipe books.

Bob Arnebeck, historian and author, for making rare documents and translations available on his Web site.

My editor, Kevin L. Lewis, for his endless enthusiasm and for believing in this book. Heather Dietz, who saw an early draft of the manuscript and made some excellent suggestions. You guys are the best.

The hundreds of kids and teachers who encouraged me to keep writing so they could find out what happened at the end of the story.

My husband, Greg, who stayed up late at night looking for comma mistakes, and who was very patient when the author became a bit bear-like.

And last, but not least, my amazing daughters, Stephanie and Meredith, for putting up with all the family trips to historical reenactments, dusty libraries, and damp cemeteries. I vow never ever to tell another chamber pot story.

Turn the page for a look at $\mathfrak{C}$hains, the first book in Laurie Halse Anderson's new trilogy.

Thursday, June 6, 1776

. . . HUNDREDS IN THIS [NEW YORK] COLONY
ARE ACTIVE AGAINST US AND SUCH IS THE WEAKNESS
OF THE GOVERNMENT, (IF IT CAN DESERVE THE NAME)
THAT THE TORIES OPENLY PROFESS THEIR SENTIMENTS
IN FAVOUR OF THE ENEMY, AND LIVE UNPUNISHED.
—LETTER OF WILLIAM TUDOR,
WASHINGTON'S CHIEF LEGAL OFFICER, TO JOHN ADAMS

WAS STUCK ON THE BACK STEPS WITH a pile of dull knives and a whetstone. It was a dreary job. First, spit on the stone. Next, hold the knife at the proper angle and circle it against the stone; ten to the left, ten to the right, until the blade was sharp enough to slice through a joint of beef like it was warm butter.

As I sharpened, I imagined using the knife to cut through the ropes that tied us to New York. I'd slice through the ocean and part the sea, and Ruth and me would walk on the sand all the way home. *Ten circles to the left . . .*

Ruth was abovestairs, standing by whilst Madam prepared herself for company. The master was locked in his library. Becky was somewhere in the crowd watching General Washington parade down Broadway with five regiments of soldiers. The sounds of beating drums and whistling fifes, and the cries of "Huzzah! Huzzah!" blew toward me over the rooftops.

I pushed everything out of my mind, save my task. *Ten cir-cles to the right . . .*

Becky came back from the parade an hour later, overflowing with stories. She nattered on about the spectacle whilst assembling the tea things for Madam and Lady Seymour, who had come again to call. I pretended to listen. Truth be told, I didn't notice when she left carrying the tray.

Ten circles to the left, ten circles to the righty, all make the blade sharp and mighty. Ten circles to the left, ten to the right . . .

Becky called for me twice before I heard her proper. Her voice was high and tight. ". . . I said to hurry! You want to get me put on the street? Madam wants you in the parlor."

The knife near slipped from my hands. "Is it Ruth?"

"No, the Lady Seymour wants to see you. And the master just arrived with gentlemen friends all calling for food and drink. Hurry!"

I washed up in the cold water bucket, quickly pinned on a clean apron, checked my kerchief was on proper and followed Becky to the parlor. She rapped lightly on the door and pushed it open. "The new girl, ma'am," she said, setting a plate of fresh-baked strawberry tarts on the table.

"Show her in," Madam said.

Becky waved at me to enter.

Madam and an older woman sat at the table, but my eyes were drawn behind them, to my sister, dressed up as Madam's pretty pet in a bleached linen shift, a navy-blue brocade short gown, and a full skirt patterned with lilacs. When she saw me, she clenched her hands together and bit her lower lip. Her eyes were red and swollen with crying.

My belly went funny and my mind raced. Why had she been crying? Was she sick? Scared? Did Madam hurt her?

Becky poked me gently in the back. This was not the time for questions.

I quickly dropped into a curtsy, bowing my head. When I stood up, the older woman, the lady aunt with all the money, gave me a shadow of a smile. She was smaller than Madam and wore a silk gown the color of a mourning dove and gray lace gloves. Her hair was curled high and powdered snow white. A necklace set with black stones shone from her neck. There were deep lines at the corners of her eyes and around her mouth, but I couldn't tell if they were from laughing or from crying.

She turned in her chair and looked at Ruth, then back at me. "And these two girls are the sisters?" she asked.

Madam reached for a tart. "That's what the man said."

The older woman sipped her tea. "What is your name, girl?" she asked me.

"Isabel, ma'am," I said. "Isabel Finch."

"Ridiculous name," Madam said. She opened her fan and waved it in front of her face. "You are called Sal Lockton now. It's more suitable."

I forced myself to breathe in slow and regular instead of telling her that my name was not her affair. "Yes, ma'am."

She glanced at my feet. "And you must wear your shoes. This is a house, not a barn."

Ruth stepped out of her corner. "Isabel."

Madam snapped the fan shut and rapped it against the edge of the table, startling us all. "What did I tell you about silence?" she said roughly.

Ruth raised one shaking finger to her mouth and said, "Shh."

"Precisely." Madam set the fan in her lap and reached for a piece of sugar with silver tongs. When she plopped it in the cup, the tea overflowed into the saucer.

Ruth stood there like a carved statue, her finger still held to her lips. I took another breath, slower than the first, and tried not to think on the newly sharpened knives on the kitchen steps. Lady Seymour curled her fingers around the teacup, her gaze marking first Madam, then Ruth, then me. She said nothing.

"Would you like Sal to serve you and Lady Seymour while I wait on the gentlemen?" Becky asked.

"Absolutely not. Show her the library and make sure the men are fed. And bring fresh tea. This has already gone cold."

We curtsied and left the parlor. Ruth's sad eyes followed me to the door.

Ten circles to the left, ten circles to the righty,
all make the blade sharp and mighty.

Back in the kitchen, Becky took a large silver tray off a high shelf in the pantry. "Hold this." She loaded the tray with plates of cold sliced tongue, cheddar cheese, brown bread, and a bowl of pickles. I could not stop thinking about the way Ruth had jumped when Madam shouted, nor the tears in her eyes.

Becky took down a second tray and set upon it four goblets, two bottles of claret wine, and a crock of mustard. She swung the kettle back over the fire to heat up more water, picked up the tray with the wine, and said, "Hop to."

I followed her to the front of the house. "But, what about my shoes?"

"The master won't notice long as he gets his grub." Becky balanced the edge of the tray on her hip and knocked on the door on the right side of the front hall. When a deep voice answered, she opened it.

Lockton looked up as we entered. "Oh, good. Sustenance," he said, pushing aside a stack of newspapers to clear off the desk.

The room was the same size and shape as the parlor, but two of the walls had bookcases built into them. A large painting of horses jumping over a high hedge hung on the third wall. A thin layer of dust lay over everything. The front windows were open, bringing in fresh air, and noise from the street entered; carts rolling over the cobblestones and church bells in the distance mingled with the voices of the four men who sat around the enormous desk.

One man looked poorer than the others; the cuffs of his coat were frayed and his hands were stained with ink. Next to him sat a man with suspicious gray eyes and a liver-colored coat with a double row of gold buttons fastened over a large pudding-belly. The third man wore something on his head that looked more like a dead possum than a wig, but his coat was crisp and new and the buckles on his shoes gleamed. The fourth was Master Lockton, looking like a cat who had just swallowed the last bite of a juicy mouse.

Becky set her tray on a sideboard. I held mine as she poured the wine and served the gentlemen. Then she had me hold the food tray so that she could serve the tongue and cheese. Talk halted as the men started in on their meal.

"Becky!" Madam called from across the hall.

"Go see to her," Lockton told Becky. "The girl can stay here. Does she know where the wine is?"

"Yes, sir," I said.

Becky and Lockton both stared at me. I had spoken out of turn. My job was to be silent and follow orders. Ruth had already learned that. *Shhhhhh* . . .

"Keep the wine flowing and the plates full," Lockton said. "My friends eat more at my table than their own."

As Becky left, Goldbuttons drained his wine, then raised his goblet. I hurried to pour him another, and topped off the drinks of the other men. Lockton gave me a curt nod when I was finished. "Stand over there," he said, pointing to the corner where the two bookshelves met each other.

I gave a wordless curtsy and took my place.

The men dove back into their conversation. "Who has been arrested because of the oath?" demanded Lockton.

"Fools unschooled in the art of fence-sitting," said Goldbuttons.

"Plank-walking, you mean," said Inkstained.

Shabbywig leaned forward and pointed his finger at Inkstained. "Don't you turn the coward on us. Not when we're this close."

"Close?" argued Inkstained. "Do you see His Majesty's ships in the harbor? I don't. I might argue that England has fled and the rebel traitors have won."

"Lower your voices," Lockton said with a scowl. He closed the windows with a loud *bang,* then returned to his seat.

"His Majesty's ships are very close, closer than you know. This rebellion will be smashed like glass under a heavy boot, and the King will be very grateful for our assistance."

The mention of the King caught my ear. I studied the wide boards on the floor and listened with care.

Goldbuttons popped a piece of cheese into his mouth and talked as he chewed. "I sincerely hope you speak the truth, Elihu. These rebel committees are multiplying faster than rabbits in the spring. They've just about ground business to a halt."

"Have they interfered with you directly?" Lockton asked.

"Every waking moment," Goldbuttons said. "The latest bit of nonsense is a Committee to Detect Conspiracies. They've sent the hounds after us, old friend."

"Have you written to Parliament? They need the specifics of our difficulties."

"Parliament is as far away as the moon," complained Inkstained.

As the other men argued about Parliament and letters of protest and counterletters and counter-counterletters, Shabbywig stabbed at the last pieces of tongue on his plate and shoved them into his mouth. He turned in his seat to look at me, held up his plate, and grunted. If I had ever done such a thing, Momma would have switched my behind for having the manners of a pig. Even Miss Mary Finch had asked with a "please" and a "thank you" when Momma served her dinner.

This is New York, I reminded myself as I crossed the room and took the plate from his hand. *The rules are different.* I loaded his plate down with the last slices of tongue and set it in front of him before retreating to my corner. *Everything is different.*

My belly growled and grumbled in its cage. The smell of the tongue and mustard and the cheese filled the room and made my mouth water. I had eaten a bowl of corn mush at breakfast and only dumplings at midday. To distract the beast in my gullet, I tried to read the names of the books on the shelves without turning my head. My eyes were as starved for words as the rest of me was for dinner.

It was hard to read from the side like that. I wanted to pull down a book, open it proper, and gobble up page after page. I wanted to stare into the faces of these men and demand they take me home. I wanted to jump on the horse in the painting and fly over the hills. Most of all, I wanted to grab my sister by the hand and run as fast as we could until the cobblestones disappeared and there was dirt under our feet again.

"Girl," Lockton said. "Bring us more bread, sliced thin. And some of Becky's apricot jam. I've missed the taste of that."

I curtsied and hurried out of the room, leaving the door open a crack so I could easily open it when I came back with my hands full. Across the hall came the quiet conversation of Madam and Lady Seymour. I paused but heard no mention of Ruth.

Shhhhh . . .

There was fresh bread on the kitchen table, but it took a piece of time to find the crock of jam. I used one of my sharp knives to slice the loaf, set out the slices on a clean plate, and put the plate and jam on a tray. It was taking me too long to finish a simple chore. I feared the master would be angry with me, and I was angry at myself for being afraid.

I was just about to push open the library door with my foot when the master said, "Compliments of His Majesty, gentleman. There's enough money here to bribe half of the rebel army."

I stopped and peered through the crack.

Madam's linen chest, the one that she had fussed about when we arrived, was in the middle of the library floor, the top thrown open. Underskirts and shifts were heaped on the floor beside it. Lockton reached into the chest and pulled out two handfuls of paper currency.

"Huzzah!" said Inkstained as Goldbuttons let out a low whistle.

"Do you have a man ready?" Lockton asked.

"Two," Shabbywig answered. "One will operate out of Corby's Tavern, the other from the Highlander."

"Good." Lockton crossed back to his desk. I could no longer see him, but his words were clear. "Every man willing to switch sides is to be paid five guineas and two hundred acres of land. If he have a wife, an additional hundred acres. Each child of his blood garners another fifty."

"Makes me want to marry the next lady I clap eyes on," Goldbuttons said.

Lockton chuckled.

I gave the door a little push and it swung open. "Sir?" I asked in a hushed tone.

"Enter," Lockton said.

I walked in. The other men did not look my way. I was invisible to them until they needed something.

"Jam," he said with a smile. "Put it right here."

I placed the tray in front of him and took my place again in the corner. The men spread the jam on the bread and drank their wine, discussing politics and war and armies over the stacks of money on my master's desk. The smell of apricots filled the warm room. It put me in mind of the orchards down the road from Miss Mary's place.

I kept my face still as a plaster mask, but inside my brain-pan, thoughts chased round and round. By the time the men rose to leave, I knew what I had to do.

How many of these award-winning books have you read?

THE UNDERNEATH
by Kathi Appelt

THE EGYPT GAME
by Zilpha Keatley Snyder

THE HEADLESS CUPID
by Zilpha Keatley Snyder

THE WITCHES OF WORM
by Zilpha Keatley Snyder

THE HOUSE OF THE SCORPION
by Nancy Farmer

SHADOW OF A BULL
By Maia Wojciechowska

JENNIFER, HECATE, MACBETH, WILLIAM MCKINLEY AND ME, ELIZABETH
by E. L. Konigsburg

THE TOMBS OF ATUAN
by Ursula K. Le Guin

THE COURAGE OF SARAH NOBLE
by Alice Dalgliesh

ONE-EYED CAT
by Paula Fox

HATCHET
by Gary Paulsen

DOGSONG
by Gary Paulsen

From
ATHENEUM

Published by
SIMON & SCHUSTER

A FINE WHITE DUST
by Cynthia Rylant

The story of one girl's unrelenting quest for freedom.

**NATIONAL BOOK
AWARD FINALIST**

**WINNER OF THE
SCOTT O'DELL AWARD
FOR HISTORICAL
FICTION**

* "Startlingly provocative . . . nuanced and evenhanded . . .
a fast-moving, emotionally involving plot."
—*Publishers Weekly*, starred review

* "Anderson explores elemental themes of power, freedom, and the
sources of human strength in this searing, fascinating story."
—*Booklist*, starred review

FROM ATHENEUM BOOKS FOR YOUNG READERS

Published by Simon & Schuster   KIDS.SimonandSchuster.com

DATE DUE

FOLLETT